"Do you have to go inside?" Lucas asked. "Couldn't we sit out here for a bit and talk?

"Talk about what?" Honey asked softly.

He shrugged, feeling like an inexperienced teenager on his first date. He'd convinced investors to take part in multimillion-dollar projects, but he had no clue how to talk his wife into spending a few minutes alone with him. Standing there barefoot, in his oldest jeans, trying to court the love of his life, Lucas felt he didn't stand a chance. "Just talk," he answered. "I didn't get to know you when I had the opportunity, it seems."

Honey drew a long, shaky breath. "We can talk inside."

"Inside?" His face went blank. "You mean in your bedroom?" When she nodded, he chuckled and leaned close. "I don't think that's a good idea, Honey. I'm afraid I wouldn't feel much like . . . talking." He laughed again, and the sound came from deep within his chest, low and husky, sending tingles along Honey's bare arms and shoulders. "When you invite a man into your bedroom, you'd better think about what you're getting yourself into," he cautioned, a wicked smile on his lips. He was teasing her, he knew, but he wasn't sure what she was asking. "It may not be safe," he added.

Honey leveled her gaze at him. "I'm a big girl, Lucas. Maybe I don't want to be . . . safe." Then she turned and walked inside, knowing he'd follow—knowing she wanted him in every sense of the word. . . .

WHAT ARE *LOVESWEPT* ROMANCES?

They are stories of true romance and touching emotion. We believe those two very important ingredients are constants in our highly sensual and very believable stories in the *LOVESWEPT* line. Our goal is to give you, the reader, stories of consistently high quality that may sometimes make you laugh, sometimes make you cry, but are always fresh and creative and contain many delightful surprises within their pages.

Most romance fans read an enormous number of books. Those they truly love, they keep. Others may be traded with friends and soon forgotten. We hope that each *LOVESWEPT* romance will be a treasure—a "keeper." We will always try to publish

LOVE STORIES YOU'LL NEVER FORGET
BY AUTHORS YOU'LL ALWAYS REMEMBER

The Editors

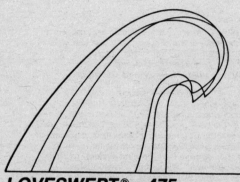

LOVESWEPT® • 475

Charlotte Hughes

Tough Guy, Savvy Lady

 BANTAM BOOKS
NEW YORK • TORONTO • LONDON • SYDNEY • AUCKLAND

TOUGH GUY, SAVVY LADY

A Bantam Book / June 1991

*If you would be interested in receiving protective vinyl
covers for your Loveswept books, please write to this address
for information:*

> Loveswept
> Bantam Books
> P.O. Box 985
> Hicksville, NY 11802

ISBN 0-553-44126-4

Published simultaneously in the United States and Canada

PRINTED IN THE UNITED STATES OF AMERICA

OPM   0 9 8 7 6 5 4 3 2 1

To Rebecca, with lots and lots of love.

Prologue

The pain in his chest was excruciating and vise-like, as though some vital organ were being squeezed and twisted. Sweat beaded on Lucas McKay's upper lip and brow as he tried to hoist himself into a sitting position on the bed.

Lucas wondered for a moment if he was dying. Surely a man could not suffer such agony and live. Hell, he was only thirty-five. Was it his heart? His father had died unexpectedly of a heart attack the year before, so it would come as no surprise to Lucas if he went the same way. He knew he didn't take care of himself. He smoked and drank and ate the wrong foods and never exercised. He lived life on the edge, as though there were no tomorrow, simply because it helped him forget. And now he was going to pay. Was he destined to die alone in bed with the smell of beer on his breath?

Lucas wondered suddenly what they would put in his obituary. His father's obituary had been no more than a few lines: "Conrad McKay, meat packer, dead at age 55." Three lines in a newspaper, the sum total of his father's sorry existence. Yet, what did he have to show for his own life? Lucas asked himself. He'd made a little money in real estate, drove an expensive car, and lived in one of Houston's fanciest condos, but that didn't mean diddly when it came right down to it. He'd failed at what really mattered—his family.

His kids would forget about him in no time, Lucas thought grimly. His ex-wife wouldn't mourn him, he knew. She'd never contacted him even once since she'd walked out on him three years earlier, except to arrange his visits with his children.

Honey Buchannan. Lucas covered his eyes and sighed, and the sound seemed to come up from the depths of his soul. He still loved her, dammit, and always would. But she had made it plain she wanted nothing more to do with him. He had called and written, had even tried to see her alone a couple of times, but couldn't get past her housekeeper, who guarded her with the zeal of a marine sergeant.

The pain rose and peaked, ripping through his chest with a knifelike clarity that all but sucked his breath away. Lucas fumbled for the telephone and dialed 911. Someone answered on the first ring.

"I need an ambulance," he said with a great deal of trouble. "I'm having a heart attack."

If awards were being handed out for fools and horses' asses, Lucas McKay figured he would get the grand prize. As he stumbled from his white

Cadillac to the door of his condo with the late morning sun glaring in his eyes, he almost wished he'd had a heart attack instead of having an ulcer.

Lucas unlocked his front door and shoved it open. The place was a mess—clothes and shoes were strewn across the floor, dirty ashtrays and dishes littered the coffee table and kitchen counter. Nobody would have suspected he'd paid a quarter of a million bucks for it.

He set the small paper sack containing his prescriptions onto the table and opened the refrigerator. The smell of soured milk and leftover pizza, one of the foods the doctor had ordered him to stay away from in the future, filled the room.

He had to do something about his life, Lucas told himself, echoing the thoughts that had haunted him all morning as he'd lain naked on that metal table awaiting test results. He walked into the bathroom and splashed some cold water on his face. Lord, but he'd turned into a worthless cuss, he thought as he looked in the mirror. His dark brown hair, fringed with gray at the temples, needed trimming. His face was puffy, his brown eyes bloodshot. He was in sorry shape, and it embarrassed him because he'd always taken pride in his appearance.

Lucas stumbled into the bedroom and sat on the edge of the bed, his gaze automatically going to the pewter frame on the nightstand, where the images of a tow-headed boy and girl stared back at him. He missed them. He missed their sweetness and innocence, the simple joy they derived from just being alive.

Sometime later, Lucas stood, his mind made up. He refused to live as he had for the past three years. He was going to Sweetbriar, Texas—to move there, if necessary. He was going to get his family back.

He was going to make Honey McKay fall in love with him all over again.

One

The Buchannan mansion, peeking out from among a throng of tall pines, hundred-year-old live oaks, and sweet gum and magnolia trees, looked much the same to Lucas. It was as stately and imposing as an aged movie queen, he thought, who, though she'd lost some of her sparkle, was well aware of her station in life. Lucas remembered the first time he'd seen the mansion as a child. Sitting in the back of his daddy's pickup truck, he'd glanced at the pink-brick residence from a distance. He'd known then and there that God had not created men equal. Why would one man be allowed to go to bed hungry at night while another had more than he needed? Major Buchannan must have been made of something different, he'd thought, and from that moment on he'd been determined to find out what it was.

Lucas parked his car in the circular drive flanked with rosebushes that looked tired and wilted in the August heat, and he gazed at the house where his ex-wife and children now lived. His heart pounded against his rib cage like conga drums. Were they happy? he wondered. How would they react when they saw him? He still remembered the first time he'd laid eyes on Honey Buchannan. Elegant in a yellow linen dress and matching hat, she'd been holding her rich daddy's hand at a political rally in town. He'd decided on the spot that he had to have her.

Squaring his shoulders, Lucas climbed out of his car, crossed the gravel drive, and made his way up the steps to the veranda, where antique rockers pickled with age swayed gently in a hot breeze that carried red dust from the pastures surrounding the house. Lucas could taste the grit in his throat as he knocked on the front door. A moment later it was opened by Honey's unsmiling housekeeper, Vera Styles.

Lucas shifted uncomfortably as the woman assessed him without emotion. She hadn't changed much, he noted. She appeared untouched by the heat. As always her iron-gray hair was pinned neatly at her nape, her apron was as crisp and white as the fat clouds that scuttled overhead. He wondered for a moment how old Vera was as he gazed at her face. Her gray eyes were alert. Alert, yet cautious.

"Hello, Vera," he said, offering the closest thing he had to a smile. In response, she sniffed and drew herself up as though she smelled something bad. "Is Honey in?" he asked.

"No."

Lucas shifted again. "How about the kids? Are they around?"

"No."

Lucas suppressed a grin. So Vera was going to play hardball. "Mind telling me where they are?"

"Todd and Melissa are at church camp for two weeks. They left just yesterday."

Lucas knew a moment of intense disappointment. He'd really had his heart set on seeing his kids, and now it looked as though he would have to wait a bit longer.

"And Mrs. McKay is at work," she added.

Lucas arched one brow. He'd never known Honey to work a day in her life, other than the charity fundraising she did. Not that she hadn't wanted to work. It's all they had argued about during their last year of marriage. "Where does she work?" he asked.

"You here to make trouble, Mr. McKay?" Vera stacked her fleshy arms beneath breasts that sagged like two water-filled balloons.

"No, no," he said quickly. "I just want to ask Honey about seeing the kids when they get back, that's all." Lucas wondered why he was going to such lengths to appease the woman, but the truth was, he'd always had a great deal of respect for Vera, despite her obvious dislike toward him. She'd started working for the Buchannans before Honey had been born, had raised the little girl when her mother had died after a lingering illness. And he knew that although Vera could wilt a vase of lilies with that stern look of hers, she could be just as loving and caring as the best of them. She loved Todd and Melissa with the same fierceness with which she loved Honey.

Vera studied him for a moment, hitching her head to the side like a chicken watching a fat caterpillar near the henhouse, ready to pounce if the mood struck. She wrinkled her nose and sniffed again, but surprised him by answering, "Mrs. McKay owns a nursery on the outskirts of town. Near Smithfield Lake."

Lucas nodded. "Thanks, Vera." He turned to go.

Vera crossed the porch and stopped. "You make any trouble for the missus, and you're going to have to answer to me, Lucas McKay," she called out in a matter-of-fact tone.

Lucas paused at the bottom of the steps and angled a glance at the woman. Her lips were pulled into a tight pucker as though she'd just sucked the insides out of a tart lemon. He grinned. "Nice seeing you again, Vera. Maybe we'll have lunch sometime." She responded with a snort.

Vera stared for a long time at Lucas's Cadillac as it disappeared down the drive. "Lord, I hope I didn't go and do the wrong thing," she said aloud.

Honey Buchannan McKay drummed her fingers on the battered metal desk as her partner read the figures from the ledger their accountant had prepared. His tone was as bleak as a cold December sky.

"It's bad, Honey," he said, his Swedish accent thicker than usual. "I don't see how we're going to make it."

Honey sighed heavily and reached for the book. "Let me see, Eric," she said. She scanned the neat column of figures. It was more serious than she'd thought. Their second summer in business, they'd not done as well as their first.

"We're broke, Honey," Eric said. "We can't cover this month's shipments, and in another month the weather will turn cool and business will be worse than it is now."

"I can't put any more money into this place," she said. "I've already used most of my trust. I've sold everything except the house and furniture. I can't let that go," she said softly.

"I'd never ask you to," Eric said, sinking onto the cracked leather sofa on the other side of the room.

"We'll just have to cut costs. Again," she added grimly. The thought that they might have to give up after all they'd been through was more than she could stand at the moment. "Which reminds me, you and I still have a truck to unload." And that reminded her of how badly her back already ached from the manual labor she'd been forced to do since letting their last two employees go. And if things didn't improve fast, they'd have to lay off Betsy, the cashier.

Eric shrugged. "Something will come up." But he didn't sound convinced.

A few minutes later, Eric and Honey exited the office, still discussing their plight. They were so immersed in the discussion, they didn't see the white Cadillac steal away from the front of the building.

When he arrived back at his hotel twenty minutes later, Lucas was still reeling from the conversation he'd overheard—and from seeing Honey again, even though he'd only caught a glimpse. Damn, but she'd looked good!

He wouldn't have recognized her on the street, what with the drastic changes in her appearance. What had happened to the prim pageboy she'd worn for as long as he'd known her? he wondered. Her hair looked wild now, tumbling past her shoulders in fat, unruly curls that made his fingers itch to touch it. And what about her clothes? She'd looked nothing like the woman who'd walked out of divorce court three years before wearing a Dior suit and Gucci shoes. Her faded denims had bordered on being indecent, they were so tight. And who the hell was Eric, the tall Scandinavian in her office who'd looked like something come down from Mount Olympus? he wondered. Whoever he was, Honey had felt comfortable enough discussing her money problems with him.

Lucas didn't like it one bit.

The first thing he did when he returned to his room was call an old friend of his who worked at the Sweetbriar Savings and Loan. In a roundabout way Lucas was able to get his friend to admit that Honey Buchannan was flat broke. Lucas could hardly believe his ears. He thanked his friend, promised to buy him a couple of beers soon, and hung up the telephone.

Lucas sat on the edge of the bed and pondered all he'd learned. The Buchannan dynasty had not crumbled overnight, it seemed. It had begun almost six years before, when Major's oil investments had turned sour. But Major had refused to face up to it, believing as always that Texas oil was liquid gold, and by the time he'd pulled out it had been too late. Lucas was almost thankful the old buzzard had lived long enough to witness the fall of his empire. Perhaps there was justice in this world after all.

Lucas was amazed he hadn't had an inkling of Major's financial trouble. And Honey, once she'd claimed her inheritance, had never told him. Of course, they had been separated by the time she would have discovered it. Honey had stayed behind after her father's funeral, had told Lucas she had to sort through his things. Lucas had assumed she'd been merely sorting through her father's belongings. She had become an heiress, and he'd figured it would take a couple of weeks to get things under control. He'd had no idea she'd been sorting through her life and marriage. Two weeks later he'd received divorce papers.

Lucas sat up late into the night planning his move and wishing more than once he had a cigarette. He hadn't smoked or drunk since leaving the hospital, and he'd taken his medication just as his doctor had prescribed. Although he felt better physically, he was a wreck emotionally. How could he have suspected that seeing Honey again after all this time would rattle him so?

Lucas awoke early the next morning and called the real estate office where he'd once worked before he'd made it big with Major Buchannan's help. Max, his old boss, answered, sounding both surprised and delighted to hear from him.

"I want to buy a house in Sweetbriar," Lucas told the man once they'd exchanged pleasantries. "Something large enough for a family. I'll pay cash, but I want to move in immediately. I'd be willing to rent while the deal goes through."

The following day, Lucas McKay arranged to purchase a sprawling Victorian farmhouse with a massive wraparound porch and old-fashioned stained-glass windows. Although the house needed painting both inside and out, it was structurally sound. Lucas was more than satisfied. He could just imagine his family there. But the grass was dead as processed hay, the rosebushes spindly with black spot, and the shrubs surrounding the house looked as though they'd simply lost the will to live.

"It's perfect," Lucas told Max, and drew out his checkbook. "I'll move in right away."

The next day, Lucas had the entire yard bulldozed.

When Lucas called Honey's office two days later, Betsy Clemmons, the cashier, answered. "I just bought the old farmhouse on Rutts Road," Lucas said without preamble. "The yard's a mess. I'll throw in a bonus if Mrs. McKay can come this afternoon and give me an estimate on the work."

Honey's pickup truck bounced over the pockmarked road, rattling her garden supplies in the back as she drove. Her blue eyes were troubled. She didn't like it one bit, she decided, going to meet a strange man in the middle of nowhere, when he hadn't even bothered to give Betsy his name. Eric wouldn't like it either, she knew, and had he not been delivering sod in the next county, he would have insisted on going with her. Betsy had offered to accompany her, but Honey didn't want to have to close the store and risk losing business.

Honey saw the farmhouse from a distance and thought the yard around it looked like a war zone. The entire area had been ripped up, every blade of grass and shrub or bush was gone, leaving only the trees. The house, with its charming gingerbread design, couldn't have looked more out of place in an asphalt parking lot.

Honey pulled into the driveway and parked beside a new white Cadillac. She made her way up the front walk to the porch, shaking her head once again at the dismal yard.

Honey paused, wishing whoever was inside would come to the door so she wouldn't have to go in. "Hello?" she called out. "Is anybody home?" When had she become so paranoid? she wondered. It was Vera's fault, she thought. Vera, who made a point of reading every grisly story from the newspaper to her. Hearing footsteps, Honey thought about turning and running, but a moment later the door was thrown open, and a tall man stepped out onto the porch. And Honey realized he was more dangerous than anyone she could have imagined.

"Hello, Honey," he said.

All she could do was stand there and stare at the man before her and note the erratic pounding of her heart and wild pitching of her stomach. It was like a bad dream—the raw landscape, the oppressive heat, the house looking so forlorn against the raw earth, and Lucas standing there smiling at her intimately.

She decided he was still about as handsome as they came, wearing charcoal slacks and a white pullover that emphasized his tanned complexion. There was a little more gray at his temples now, she noted, but it only enhanced his dark good looks and added an air of sophistication.

"Lucas?" she said, her voice trembling from the sheer shock of seeing him again. "What are you doing here?"

Lucas crossed the porch and descended the steps slowly, never taking his eyes off the woman before him. How many times had he rehearsed this scene in his mind? he wondered. How many times had he dreamed of looking into those eyes again, eyes that could sparkle like precious blue stones when she was happy and turn smoky in passion. But now, now that she was actually standing there in the flesh with her hair like ripened wheat fluttering in the warm breeze, he didn't quite know what to say.

"I've come home, Honey," was all he could think of.

Honey blinked once, twice, trying to absorb what he was saying. "What do you mean you've come home? You left Houston?"

"This is my home now," he said, indicating the house behind him with one sweeping gesture.

Honey took a step back, not really knowing what to do or say next. Vera had told her Lucas had come by, and they'd both been surprised that he hadn't called back, even more so that he hadn't shown up at her place of business. "What's going on, Lucas?" she asked, her eyes suddenly wary. "Is this some kind of joke? Why are you really here?"

Lucas closed the distance between them, coming to a halt only inches in front of her. He studied the delicate lines of her face, thinking she had never looked lovelier, her complexion the color of a ripe peach in the sun. The jeans she wore were soft with a cottony sheen, no doubt from years of laundering. They were snug, complimenting her feminine figure. He smiled at the small frayed hole at her knee. He was seeing a side of Honey he'd never seen before, and he liked it.

"I want my family back, Honey," he said simply, his gaze creeping upward, past her white cotton blouse, which looked as crisp as a September morning. He ached to take her into his arms, bury his face where her collar lay open and exposed skin that looked as delicate as rose petals. "And I don't much care what I have to do to get them," he added.

"Your children are away at the moment."

"I'm not talking about my children, and you know it."

His response made her head spin. "You've really lost it this time, Lucas," she said. "If you think for one minute that I could . . . that we could . . ."

"I've given you three years to come to your senses, Honey," he said.

"Come to my senses!"

"But you refused to face the fact that you're still in love with me."

"Oh, Lucas, you truly *are* a sick man."

"So I'm going to plant myself right here in Sweetbriar, and I'm not going to budge until you realize you can't live without me."

Honey was aghast. He was so close, she could smell his after-shave, feel the heat from his body, see the golden specks in his brown eyes. She wanted to back away, but her feet were solidly glued to the sidewalk beneath her. "Is that what all this is about?" she asked. "Is that why you bought this place?"

"Maybe."

"Then you really are crazy if you think I'm going to do business with you. I thought I made it plain three years ago that I have nothing more to say to you."

"I've changed, Honey."

"Baloney."

"And I'm going to prove it to you. I'm going to show you once and for all that I can be the kind of husband and father you want."

"I don't want a husband, Lucas," she said, feeling close to hysteria now. She was angry. She had truly counted on bringing in new business, hoping to ease her and Eric's financial worries. Now she realized what a waste of time making the drive out had been. "Why should I want a man in my life to tell me when to make my every move?" she demanded. "I like my life, Lucas. I'm content making my own decisions, coming and going as I please. Now, do us both a favor and go back to Houston where you belong." She turned to leave, but she was prevented from doing so when his hand closed around one wrist.

"Not so fast, Honey."

Honey twirled around on her heels, and the look in her eyes was intense. "Take your hands off me, Lucas McKay," she said, her voice little more than a whisper.

Lucas was clearly surprised. "Would you calm down, for Pete's sake."

"Let go of me!"

He released her. "You used to enjoy having me touch you, Honey," he said. "Remember?" Her expression told him that she did remember. "And I knew exactly where to touch you, didn't I? I knew how to make you feel good all over. And I still do," he added softly. "One of these days, and sooner than you think, you're going to ask me to touch you again." He said it with the confidence of a man used to getting exactly what he wanted.

Honey was on the verge of tears, and it made her even angrier. How could Lucas walk into her life after three years and stir up feelings she'd thought long dead? He could still get to her; he knew the right buttons to push. And yes, he'd known exactly where to touch her and how. The memory was unsettling. He'd discovered long ago all the pleasure spots that made her shiver: the sensitive skin between her toes and fingers; the nape of her neck where the downy hairs prickled each time he caressed her there with his lips, his warm breath fanning her earlobes and shoulders. Her stomach fluttered at the thought of those same lips skimming the backs of her knees, the small of her back, her thighs, which he claimed had the texture of satin. She had convinced herself she was better off without him, had even learned not to need him, but she would never forget what it was like to lie naked in his arms or watch his eyes smolder as he made love to her.

It took several moments for Honey to get her emotions under control. When she did, she hitched her head high and stared him coolly in the eye. "I can't tell you where or where not to live, Lucas," she finally said, her voice unsteady. "If you've made up your mind to move back to Sweetbriar, that's your business. And you're welcome to see Todd and Melissa when they return. But leave me out of it, Lucas." This time when she turned to go, he didn't try to stop her.

"What about my yard?" he asked.

"Find someone else."

Lucas watched her climb into her pickup truck

and drive off down the dusty road. For a long time, he merely stood there, wondering what he could have done to make her despise him. Did she hate him so much that she would risk losing everything she had to keep from having to work with him?

Two

Honey told Eric about her encounter with Lucas when he returned that afternoon. "I feel like I've let everybody down," she said. "We stood to make a lot of money on the job, but I just couldn't put my personal feelings aside."

Eric, sweaty from the work he'd done, stripped off his T-shirt and wiped his chest and forehead. "Don't be ridiculous," he said. "I don't expect you to do something you don't feel comfortable with." He sank onto the old leather sofa and crossed his legs. "Besides, we're making money on this sod deal, you know. If everything goes all right, we could get this developer's business and do all his landscaping in the future." When Honey didn't answer, he went on. "You're still carrying a torch for this guy, aren't you?" he said.

"Is it that obvious?" she asked glumly.

"It's written all over your face, kiddo. What are you going to do about it?"

"Stay as far away from him as possible."

"That won't be easy with him living in the same town, you know. You're bound to run into him sooner or later."

Honey knew it was true. In a town the size of Sweetbriar it was inevitable that she would see Lucas from time to time. She had effectively avoided his telephone calls and letters over the past three years, but there would be no escaping him now, especially if he intended to see the children more often. In the past, she had arranged his visits through Vera, but she knew she couldn't count on her housekeeper always being available to take care of it. Besides, it was cowardly to expect someone else to do all her dirty work. She sighed. It had been so much easier with Lucas living in Houston. What bothered her most, of course, was her own reaction to him. She had mentally bundled up her feelings for him a long time ago and tucked them away, hoping one day they would somehow miraculously wither into nothingness. But they hadn't. They were as potent and dangerous as ever.

"Sometimes it's better to face up to those things that frighten us most," Eric said after a moment. "You've come a long way in the past three years, Honey. Surely your ex-husband doesn't have that much control over you now."

"You think I should take the job, don't you, Eric?"

"That's up to you. But you're never going to break free of this man until you stop running from him."

Honey pondered it, knowing Eric's words made complete sense. One of the things she liked about him was that he was so levelheaded. While she might fret over a decision for hours, simply because she'd never made a whole lot of them in her life, Eric calmly laid them out and examined all the issues before choosing a solution. She had learned a lot from him. She cherished his friendship, his ability to discuss a problem rationally with her without trying to tell her what to do. And once she made her decision, he always supported her, whether it turned out to be the right one or not. But what she valued even more were the times he'd come to her for advice. She could not remember when anyone had actively sought her opinion. Only rarely had Lucas ever confided his business troubles to her, and she'd never known if he'd taken her suggestions seriously or not.

She knew in her heart the correct decision. But how could she possibly work with Lucas McKay on a daily basis? she wondered. It would not be easy. She couldn't imagine looking at him without experiencing deep emotion. She'd be reminded of how he'd looked in passion, his eyes black as pitch, his lips full and greedy as they captured hers; how he'd looked when she'd given birth to their children, those same eyes soft and caring and so proud she thought he'd burst.

Divorcing Lucas had been the toughest thing she'd ever done in her life, tougher than losing her mother at a young age and tougher than living with an overprotective father who'd ruled with an iron fist and had made even her simplest decisions for her. But divorcing Lucas had been as necessary as marrying him had been. She had run away with Lucas to escape a domineering father, only to find she'd traded one source of control for another. No wonder Lucas hadn't been afraid to stand up to

Major, she thought. He was just like the man, cut from the same cloth.

But she had come a long way, Honey reminded herself. She had rebuilt her life and was more content than she'd been in years. Her children were happy and thriving, no doubt a result of her own emotional well-being. She had money problems, of course, but she would get through them. She had confidence in herself, and she wouldn't let Lucas strip it from her—no matter what.

"I'll do the job," Honey said finally. She'd start right away, she thought, while Todd and Melissa were away at camp. She didn't want them involved. "I'll drive back out there and take care of it the way I should have in the first place."

Eric looked pleased. "You want me to go with you?"

"No, I'll be okay."

He grinned and nodded. "Good girl. Show him what you're made of."

When Honey returned to Lucas's place a while later, she found him dragging battered furniture from his attic. "Mind if I come in?" she asked when he didn't invite her right away.

"What's wrong, did you forget your garden tools?" he asked, sarcasm slipping into his voice as he stepped back to admit her. His mood was as sour as spoiled milk after their earlier conversation. What could she possibly want now? Perhaps there were still a few insults she wanted to toss in his face. His mood hadn't improved when he discovered most of the "antiques" left behind by the previous owners were nothing more than worthless junk, including the kitchen appliances. He'd cussed himself unmercifully when he'd checked them out. After all his years in real estate he should've known to look first. He simply hadn't been thinking. Nevertheless, he was surprised to see Honey.

Honey noticed he'd changed into work clothes, old jeans and a short-sleeve cotton shirt that hung open to his waist and exposed part of his chest. His black chest hair glistened, and it took all the willpower she could muster to keep from staring at it. Surely there was not a man alive with broader shoulders, she decided.

"No, I came back to see if we could work something out," she answered, trying to force her voice to remain calm. "If you're still interested in having some landscape work done, I'd like to apply for the job." When he didn't respond, she went on. "But first, I'll have to set some ground rules."

Lucas arched one dark brow. "Such as?"

"We put our personal differences aside. And I don't want an instant replay of what happened earlier." There, she'd said it, laid it on the line, so to speak. Now it was up to Lucas to make the final decision, but she could draw satisfaction knowing she had given him a choice, that she had not merely tucked her tail and run. There was some small part of her that wished he would turn down her offer, despite the fact she and Eric needed the business. She was not ready to put herself through an emotional wringer just to get the work.

After a moment, Lucas nodded. "I was way out of line earlier, Honey, and I'm sorry." And he was sorry, he thought, sorry that she was so desperate for money that she was *forced* to deal with him. He wondered for a moment if her friend Eric had insisted she do it, and the thought irritated him. He would never have forced her into something merely for money. He could scrape and grovel for a living if he had to, if it meant feeding his family, but Honey was above all that. Still, she was as proud as her father had been and any attempt he made to help her would only drive a wedge deeper between them.

Lucas's apology surprised Honey and made her uneasy. He didn't do it often, she knew, mainly because he always thought he was right. Lucas McKay never did anything unless he had a reason. But she didn't have time to think about it, she needed her wits about her. Instead, she offered him a hopeful smile. "I accept your apology, Lucas," she said. "I think if you're going to live here and see the children on a regular basis, we should at least try to be friends."

He couldn't thing of anything that sounded less appealing, but he didn't say as much. "How are the kids, Honey?"

"They're fine. Todd starts third grade this year, you know, and Melissa goes into first. They've made a lot of friends here, in school and at church. And Todd is playing ball this year."

"Is he any good?"

She nodded. "Eric, my business partner, practices with him a lot."

That explained who the man in her office was, Lucas thought, but he couldn't help but wonder if Eric was more than just a partner. It irritated him to know another man played ball with his son when he'd had very little opportunity even to see the boy the past few years.

"And Melissa wants to take dance lessons," Honey went on. "She looks more like you every day, Lucas."

"You don't say."

"And she has your temper," Honey added with a laugh. "I can't begin to tell you the trouble it gets her into."

Lucas frowned. "That's probably because nobody understands her."

"Her kindergarten teacher seems to think it has a lot to do with her being spoiled," she said, amused that Lucas would go to bat for Melissa when he didn't even know the circumstances.

"I see Vera is as crotchety as ever," he said.

"She never changes."

Lucas couldn't think of anything else to say. Honey wasn't interested in knowing how much he'd missed her, he realized. He'd missed her in his bed and in his life, missed the way she looked in the morning, her body warm and flushed from sleep. He'd simply missed loving her, something he'd taken for granted before their divorce. And now that she was so close that he could reach out and take her in his arms, he had to hold back. That was what really hurt, he decided. He was a man who had always taken what he wanted in the past, and now he couldn't.

"Well, I suppose I ought to show you around outside," he said. Lucas walked beside her to the front door and held it open, careful to keep his distance. The last thing he wanted to do was scare her off.

Once they stepped outside, Honey shook her head at the grim sight. "Did you do this, Lucas?"

When he nodded, she added, "Don't you think it was a bit drastic?"

"The grass was dead. I thought I'd put seed down, but then I realized I didn't know how to go about it, and I didn't want to have to wait that long for it to come up." He knew he wasn't being completely honest, but if Honey found out he'd gone to such extremes to see her again, she might very well think he'd lost his mind. He was already beginning to suspect as much himself.

"You want it sodded, then?"

"Yeah."

"That's expensive."

"Money is no problem." He regretted it the minute he said it. With Honey having financial problems, the last thing he wanted to do was flaunt his own wealth. At the same time, he wanted her to know he could afford to help her. He hated playing these games with her, he thought. Why couldn't he just go to her bank and make a substantial deposit? It was difficult to remain patient when his family was in trouble.

Honey walked down the steps and perused her surroundings. "What happened to your shrubs?"

"I had them taken up too. They were worthless. And the rosebushes had some kind of disease, I think. I want the whole place landscaped, Honey. And I want one of those fancy gardens, maybe even with a fish pond. Someplace peaceful where I can sit at the end of the day and . . . meditate."

This amused her. "Meditate? Since when have you had time for that?"

"I'm sort of semiretired. I've got plenty of time on my hands to meditate. Among other things," he added, the corners of his lips twitching so that

Honey had no doubt what those other things might be. She blushed and turned away.

"Lucas, I can't see you sitting around for very long," she finally said, kneeling and taking a clump of dirt in one hand. "You'd climb the walls in no time." She couldn't help but wonder what he'd done with his real estate company, his very lifeblood. But she wouldn't ask. To do so would only pave the way for personal involvement, and she was determined to keep their dealings on a professional level.

"Like I said, Honey, I've changed."

She didn't respond. Lucas knelt beside her, watching her play with the dirt in her slender hand. She squeezed it lightly, and his gut tightened at the sight of the flexing motion and the thoughts it evoked. He imagined that hand, both hands, roaming freely over his body, stroking and squeezing. Lucas shook his head slightly to block the images.

Honey opened her fist and studied the dirt closely. "We'll want to check your pH balance and do a couple of soil samples," she said. "Before we sod the place, I'd suggest adding a few nutrients to the soil. We want to insure its success." She paused, uncomfortably aware he was watching her. "In the meantime, you can select any trees or shrubs you'd like to use. I'll be glad to work up a diagram for you after I have a look around."

"How long is all this going to take?"

"It won't take more than a few days, unless you plan to get extravagant with that garden of yours. The one you plan to use for meditating," she added with a trace of a smile.

Lucas stood and shoved his hands in his pockets. He needed more than just a few days to win Honey back. "But I *had* planned to be a little extravagant with my garden, Honey," he said. "As well as the yard. It's important to me, you know. And I was sort of thinking I'd like to have a play area for the kids when they visit. A nice one," he added, "like they have at the park."

"We can do that," she said, nodding her head enthusiastically. "You have a perfect spot over there beneath those shade trees. I know a place where you can order the playground equipment, then I'll landscape around it."

"How long will that take?"

She shrugged. "I'm not sure, but we can choose the site, and I'll work around it. I'll hurry as much as I can."

He touched her arm lightly, then pulled his hand away when her gaze turned cautious. "No, I don't want you to hurry," he said quickly. "Take your time. I don't care how long it takes as long as it's done right. And one last thing, I want you to handle this personally."

"Stop worrying, Lucas," she said, laughing for the first time since she'd arrived. Lucas had forgotten how much he enjoyed hearing that sound. "It'll be done right. Now, why don't you go inside and do what you were doing so I can get started."

"Go inside?" That wasn't in his plan at all. "But what if you have questions?"

"I'll knock on your door. You'll just be in my way out here."

"But, Honey—"

"Then, when I've finished, I'll go back to the office and draw the diagram and drop it off some-time tomorrow . . . maybe at lunch."

"Lunchtime?" His mind was already at work.

"Unless it's not convenient."

"No, no," he said quickly. "That's fine." She turned, making her way toward her pickup. Lucas studied her swaying hips as she walked. He'd liked the way her hips had filled out after Todd's birth, full and round and feminine. He'd liked the way she'd looked in the expensive lingerie she wore. While Honey often looked for sales when she shopped, she splurged when it came to underwear, buying only the finest quality. Lucas remembered how light it was, as delicate and wispy as a cobweb. He could feel himself becoming aroused simply thinking of it.

Lucas didn't get a damn thing accomplished while Honey was there. He paced the living room, stopping now and then to peer out the window at her as she inspected his grounds, making notes on a yellow legal pad from time to time. Then, without even saying good-bye, she climbed into her pickup truck and drove away.

Lucas spent the rest of the day cleaning, then wondered why he didn't pay someone to do it for him. Not that he had anything better to do, he reminded himself. He had no job. Every so often, that knowledge gnawed at his gut. Had he really put his real estate company up for sale? he asked himself disbelievingly. He remembered the years of hard work and wondered if he'd been a bit rash by putting it on the market. Even now, his attorney was probably interviewing potential investors. Of course, if the company sold for anywhere close to the asking amount, it would see him through a healthy retirement—him and Honey, he amended silently.

Lucas thought of calling his attorney to find out how things were going in Houston, then realized his telephone wouldn't be installed until the following day. So much still needed to be done. The house needed repairs, inside and out, not to mention repainting. The wood floors and windows were as grimy as a grease bucket.

Lucas pulled a canned drink from the sputtering refrigerator and took a seat at the old Formica kitchen table. He wondered again if he had screwed up royally by wanting to purchase the house. He didn't have the slightest idea how to decorate or choose furniture. He had wanted a yard, plain and simple, so he could have an excuse to see Honey. Now, he had no clue as to what he would do with the rest of the place. After a moment, he went out to his car and grabbed his briefcase, where he found a notebook. He decided to make a list.

When Honey arrived the following day at noon, the house smelled of Mexican food, and Lucas was hard at work cleaning his wood floors. "Have you got a minute to go over this diagram?" she asked, remembering suddenly she hadn't eaten all day.

"Sure." He opened the door to let her in, wondering if she had any idea how eager he'd been to see her again. "Actually, I was about to break for lunch," he said. "Won't you join me?"

She shook her head. "I don't have time."

He looked amused. "Since when are you too busy to eat Mexican food?" he asked. "As I remember, it's your favorite. I also remember spending a lot of Friday nights at the Fiesta Palace in Houston when you were pregnant," he added. "I always believed all those jalapeño peppers you ate had something to do with Todd's being born three weeks early."

Honey obliged him with an impersonal smile, but hurried on. "Lucas, if you don't mind, I'm in a bit of a rush." The last thing she wanted to think about was all those evenings she'd sat across from Lucas at the restaurant in Houston, with him teasing her that she could eat her weight in Mexican food, his eyes almost black in the candlelight. And later, in their bedroom, when he would fetch her a large glass of ice water because she would be so thirsty. More often than not, the evening would turn intimate, and they would make love long into the night. Those were her happiest memories. But once Lucas's work had started to interfere with their Friday night dates, and he spent more and more time away, it was never the same. Finally, he'd rented an apartment in the city instead of making the drive home every night. And when Honey had asked why they didn't move closer to town, he'd told her he enjoyed coming home on weekends, feeling as though he had a retreat. Honey had felt the resentment growing inside, but that's where it stayed, because she had learned long ago to keep her feelings to herself.

"You don't care if I eat while we talk, do you?" Lucas asked, interrupting her thoughts.

"No, of course not. I'll try to be brief."

"Come on in the kitchen," he said. "It should be time to pull it out of the oven."

"When did you learn to cook Mexican food?" she asked, following him into the room.

"Oh, I hired a woman to clean the house shortly after . . ." He paused. "After you and the kids moved back here. She taught me." He didn't want to have to think about those days following her departure nor the ultimate sale of their home—the home he'd purchased specifically for her. It had pained him to sell it, though he'd waited almost a year after she'd left before doing so. The upkeep had been too much for him to handle.

Lucas grabbed an oven mitt and opened the oven door. They were both assailed by the aroma of enchiladas. He closed his eyes briefly. He would pay for this, he thought, knowing he wasn't supposed to eat spicy foods. But knowing Honey's weakness for Mexican food, it might be worth it. He pulled the pan out and set it on the stove. "I think it's ready," he said. "The cheese looks bubbly enough, don't you think?"

Honey peered over his shoulder. "Yes, I think it's done," she said, her mouth watering profusely. "Now, about your yard."

"At least have a soft drink while you're here," he said, opening the refrigerator and tossing her a cold can before she could object. She caught the drink in one hand. He grinned to himself. She wouldn't last five minutes.

When Lucas had filled a plate with enchiladas, he grabbed a fork and his canned drink and joined Honey at the table. "Okay, show me what you've got," he said.

Honey thumbed through her legal pad to the diagrams she'd made of Lucas's yard, trying to ignore the smell of his food. "Okay, we have to take into consideration where your underground utilities are located as well as the overhead wires. Not to mention where you get full sun and where it's shady." She stopped to catch her breath, and her stomach growled. "I'd suggest situating a number of evergreens here on this side of the house, and maybe a few closer to your driveway."

Lucas cut into one of the enchiladas and popped a piece into his mouth. He closed his eyes and chewed. "Hmmm. Ain't nothing quite like Mexican food made from scratch," he said. "Know what I mean? 'Course, I had to go out and buy cookware and dishes and silverware in order to make it," he added with a chuckle, "but it was worth it."

". . . And I thought maybe we'd put some ornamental trees over here," Honey said, tapping her yellow pencil nervously as she talked.

"What do you mean by 'ornamental'?"

"Oh, smaller trees just to accent your yard. You can choose some with decorative bark or foliage. Maybe a couple of fruit trees if you like."

"Sounds good to me. I'd like something pretty and soft looking, maybe in pink or white."

"Well, you could select from a number of trees, Lucas," she said. "Heaven knows your lot is big enough. Perhaps you'd enjoy a cherry tree and maybe a silk. They're fairly hardy. And then, of course, you could always go with some nice flowering dogwoods. Everybody loves dogwoods. I have some catalogs in the truck you can look at."

"Naw, that'll take too long, and you said you were in a hurry."

"Well, I'm not in *that* much of a hurry," she said eagerly. This was the best part of her job as far as she was concerned, looking through the catalogs and choosing just the right tree for a particular spot. So many times, people already knew what they wanted and just ordered it from her. But with Lucas knowing so little about landscaping, she would play a big part in designing his lot. She smiled suddenly, feeling good about having taken those college courses in landscape architecture at night. "I'll get the catalog," she said, already rising from her chair.

He grinned. "And I'll fix you a plate of enchiladas." When she started to object, he stopped her. "Look, I can hear your stomach growling from across the table, Honey. Why are you making such a big deal out of this?"

She wanted to tell him, but couldn't. How could she make him understand that she didn't want to sit across a table from him and eat Mexican food as she had so many times before, didn't want to have to remember all the intimacies that one simple act had evoked? But wasn't that running from him? she asked herself. By taking on this landscaping job, she had proved to herself once and for all that she was finished running. Surely she could share an innocent lunch with the man without getting personally involved.

"Sure, I'll have lunch with you, Lucas," she finally said, smiling to ease the sudden tension between them. "And then perhaps one day Eric and I will take you to lunch." She hurried out the door for her catalogs.

Lucas shrugged, but made his way back to the stove to fix her a plate. The last thing he wanted to do was have lunch with her business partner, but for the moment he was happy to have her in the same room with him again.

• • •

Lucas decided there was something quite sexy about watching Honey eat Mexican food. She enjoyed it with such relish that it was well worth the trouble he'd gone through to prepare it. "How about a cup of coffee?" he asked, once she'd cleaned her plate.

"That sounds good to me," she said, rubbing her stomach. "By the way, that was a wonderful meal. I'll have to eat salads for a week to make up for it."

Lucas poured two cups of coffee from the new automatic coffeemaker he'd purchased when he'd bought his dishes. Once he set them down, Honey opened one of the catalogs she'd retrieved from her truck and leafed through it, pointing out trees she had in mind for his lot. Lucas moved his chair to her side of the table in order to get a closer look at the pictures, but it was all he could do to concentrate on what she was saying when he caught a whiff of her perfume. It was different, not the brand he'd selected for her personally shortly after they'd married, but he decided he liked it nevertheless.

"What made you decide to get into this line of work, Honey?" Lucas asked after a moment, enjoying the way her eyes lit up when she told him about a particular tree or shrub.

She laughed self-consciously. "I'm afraid I didn't have much experience in anything else," she said. Her expression turned rueful. "Those fancy schools Daddy sent me to didn't teach me much more than flower arrangement and social graces. There's not much of a demand for that sort of thing in the real world."

Lucas felt his gut ache at the thought of Honey having to worry about her future. That was his job, he thought glumly, to take care of and provide for her and the children. He'd clawed his way through life for as long as he could remember, and he was good at it. But he didn't want that for Honey and his children.

"What would you have liked to study?" he asked, feeling somewhat embarrassed that he'd never known. How could he have lived with her five years and had no inkling? he wondered.

She shrugged. "I wanted to be an architect. I suppose that's why this job appeals to me so much. I get to design landscapes instead of build- ings. As the business grows, I hope to be able to design entire subdivisions."

Lucas pondered her words. He knew without being told that Major had been the one who'd prevented Honey from being an architect, but he couldn't imagine why. Major had encouraged her to do charity work, he remembered, had even bragged to his clients about it. Maybe the man didn't want folks to think he couldn't provide for his daughter, that she was part of the working class. Charity work was okay as long as she wasn't forced to accept a paycheck for it. Lucas was suddenly stabbed with guilt. He had been guilty of the same crime.

"You said you wanted something soft and pretty," Honey interrupted after a moment, "and I think these double-flowering dogwoods would do the trick." She smiled, and Lucas thought she had never looked more beautiful or desirable. He wanted to take her into his arms, tell her how much he still loved her, how much he cherished her. He wanted to hold her close and kiss away her fears and troubles. Silently, he pleaded with her. *Let me help you, baby. Let me make everything all right for you.* But he wasn't sure that's what she wanted. It occurred to him that he really didn't know her at all.

Lucas looked at the glossy picture before him, trying his best to concentrate on what she was telling him about the tree. "Yes, I am definitely in the mood for something soft and pretty," he said. He glanced up and found her watching him curiously, and it was all he could do to keep from leaning over and capturing her lips with his own. He had never wanted her more than at that moment. He hurt all over for wanting her.

Much to his surprise, Honey blushed. He was surprised even more when he noticed how badly her hands trembled when she raised her coffee cup to her lips. "Are you okay?" he asked, his voice almost raw with need.

"F-fine." She blushed again.

Lucas sat back in his chair and gazed at her for a moment. "You're uncomfortable with me, aren't you?"

She laughed nervously and glanced away. "A little, perhaps."

"Why?"

She chanced a look in his direction. "That should be obvious. We're divorced now, and this is highly irregular."

"Does your . . . uh . . . nervousness have anything to do with the fact that you're still attracted to me?"

"Absolutely not."

He wasn't convinced. Male pride told him she

was not immune to him, not when he was sitting there bursting at the seams to have her. "Aw, come on, Honey, I know you better than that. You're attracted to me. Your eyes are too bright and your skin is flushed. I know the signs well."

"Stop laughing at me, Lucas," she said tersely.

"I'm not laughing just at you, darlin', I'm laughing at both of us. Because as much as we try to hide it, we are very much turned on by each other."

"Speak for yourself, Lucas," she said. "I'm just here to landscape your yard, okay?"

"And you have no desire to find out if we still sizzle when we're together."

Her face flamed. "Of course not."

"I remember a time when the two of us could char a new set of sheets in no time flat."

Honey gasped. She closed the catalog with a loud thud that made Lucas jump. "Lord, look at the time," she said. "I have to go, Lucas." She stood so quickly, she almost toppled her chair.

He chuckled. " 'Course you do."

Her head snapped up. "What's that supposed to mean?"

"It means you're running scared, Honey," he said softly, unfolding himself from the chair. He stood only inches from her, so close, he could see her pulse beating frantically at the base of her throat. He reached a finger up and touched it lightly. Honey flinched, but didn't move. He took her immobility as consent and curled his palm around her neck. Their gazes locked. "Your heart is racing like mad, darlin'—"

"Don't call me that."

"If you're so scared of me, maybe you should bring your business partner out with you next time." He was pushing her and he knew it, but patience had never been one of his virtues.

"I'm not scared of you."

"Then why the hell have you avoided me for three years, Honey?" he demanded. "You ignored my letters and phone calls, refused to see me. I'd call that scared. You know what I think?"

"I can't wait to hear it," she said, her voice tinged with sarcasm.

"I think this tough act you put on is just that. An act."

"You don't know me anymore, Lucas," she said, gathering her belongings close so that he was forced to move his hand. "I'm not the woman I was. I make my own decisions now. I answer to no one but myself."

"And I like it. It excites the hell out of me," he said. "But there's a part of you that is vulnerable to me, and you know it. You can deny it all you like, but you're only fooling yourself." His gaze caressed her lips as he spoke. "You're dying to know if I can still set you on fire. And I can, Honey. I can make you burn."

"Lucas—"

"You've never forgotten, have you? I can see by the look on your face you haven't. And that's why you've refused to see me. It was much easier to throw it all away as long as you didn't have to look at me. Otherwise, you could never have gone through with it."

"Stop it!" Honey turned away, blinking furiously as she tried to block the sensual images he had conjured up in her head. His voice, like liquid velvet, could coax her knees to putty, she knew. She headed for the door.

"What's wrong, Honey, does the truth hurt?" he asked, following behind her. He knew he had gone too far, could very well push her out of his life forever, but he couldn't back off. He'd waited three years, and now he had to confront her or lose his mind. He moved to the doorway. Her eyes flashed with panic, then anger as she tried to get around him and couldn't. "I never looked at another woman the whole time we were married, Honey. Did you know that? I never even thought about another woman."

"Because you were so wrapped up in yourself."

"I was wrapped up in being a success. I wanted to give you the things you'd always had. I wanted to measure up in your eyes. The only way I knew how to do it was to work my tail off. And I did give you beautiful things. A nice house—"

"A lovely prison."

"Prison!" He almost spat the word.

"That's right, Lucas. A prison. I had no life. I existed only for you—to bear your children, entertain your clients, and warm your bed."

"Oh, it never occurred to me you didn't enjoy being in my bed."

"It wouldn't have."

For a moment, Lucas felt as though she'd slapped him. "So, now you're telling me you didn't like sleeping with me, huh?" he said, gritting his teeth. He was trembling now, his emotions spewing forth as raw and naked as his yard outside. Three years of want and need and yearning had taken its toll. "Well, maybe you've forgotten what it was like between us, lady. Maybe you need a reminder."

"Don't do this, Lucas." Honey could feel her eyes

stinging with tears, but before she could say anything else, Lucas's mouth came down on hers. For
a moment all she could do was stand there as his
lips took hers with a fierceness and hunger she
had never known, not even in five years of marriage. He crushed her against his wide chest, the
hard lines of his body making her very much
aware of his masculinity. Her head spun wildly as
he prodded her lips open to receive his tongue.
Lucas backed her against the door with his hips.

Lucas knew his control was slipping as his
tongue plunged inside Honey's mouth, tasting
again the sweetness he'd never forgotten. He
wanted her with a desperation he'd never known,
and as the kiss deepened he realized he would
have no qualms about taking her there on the
floor. He was losing it, he thought, and it frightened him that another human being could rob
him so easily of his steely control.

Lucas raised his head and sucked his breath in
sharply, filling his lungs with desperately needed
oxygen. That was the only excuse he had for his
present state—the way his body shook and felt
weak all over as though he'd just stepped off a wild
carnival ride. But he froze when he glanced down
and found himself looking into Honey's luminous
eyes. The sight of her tears hit his gut like a chunk
of hot metal.

"I made you cry," he said, his expression taking
on a dazed look. He hated himself for the sudden
relief that spread over him at seeing them, relief at
knowing he could get to her after all this time. She
was not totally immune to him.

"Like hell you did," she said, tilting her head up
proudly, but the tears fell freely and mocked her

denial. She was so angry, she could barely speak. "Are you happy now, Lucas?" she managed, her voice trembling as badly as her knees. "That's the trouble with you, you always take what you want from people whether they're willing to give or not. That's what you are, Lucas, a taker."

"I have a hell of a lot to give now, Honey," he said, wondering how his voice could sound so controlled when he was a nervous wreck.

"You don't know the first thing about giving," she said. "You're just like my father. You're so consumed with your own self-importance, you can't see that the people around you have needs."

"I'm not your father!" he snapped. "I'm your husband. And I could be a damn good one now if you'd let me."

"You are *not* my husband. I divorced you, remember?"

He gave a snort. "That doesn't mean squat to me, Honey, and you know it. You could divorce me a dozen times, but in your heart you know we belong together. You can deny it all you want, but sooner or later you're going to realize the truth. Then maybe we can go on with our lives." He stepped closer, and when he spoke again, his voice was almost tender. "Let's put all this behind us, baby. The last thing I want to do is be cruel to you. But I'll do what I have to in order to get you back."

Much to his surprise, Honey smiled. "I think you underestimate me, Lucas. Maybe you've forgotten who I am."

Lucas was taken off guard. "What are you talking about?"

"I'm Major Buchannan's daughter, remember? I may not be as loud and obnoxious as he was, or throw my weight around, but there's an awful lot of him in me that I didn't even know existed until three years ago."

"What are you trying to say, Honey?"

"That I'm not a pushover, Lucas, and you're not going to just waltz into my life and tell me how it's going to be. Is that clear?" When he didn't answer, she pulled a slip of paper from her legal pad and handed it to him. "Here's a rough estimate of what it'll cost to have us landscape your lot. If you're interested, call my office and make an appointment like everybody else." She turned and pushed through the door.

Lucas, not knowing what to say, followed her out the door and stood dumbly on the front porch as she made her way to her pickup. He watched as she pulled out of the driveway and her truck disappeared from sight.

He was thoroughly and utterly dumbstruck. What had happened to the woman he'd married eight years ago? Getting her back wasn't going to be an easy task, he thought.

Lucas muttered a curse and went back into the house. His stomach was on fire from all the Mexican food he'd eaten.

Three

Sweetbriar, Texas, had changed very little over the years, Lucas noted as he drove through the sleepy little town early the following morning on his way to see Honey. Folks moved at a much slower pace, stopping to chat with friends and neighbors as they readied for business, sweeping the sidewalks in front of their stores, and polishing display windows.

Lucas still remembered how scared people had been when Sweetbriar had been selected as the site for the large distribution warehouse. Close to one hundred new families had moved into the area. They said the town would never be the same, and Lucas had felt somewhat guilty that he'd had a hand in planning it. He'd never considered whether the townspeople wanted it; hell, the worst it could do was provide jobs and upgrade schools, he'd thought. Of course, the fact that he'd made a fortune himself on the deal was a big factor in his decision, but he honestly figured the changes would do the town good.

And he *had* made a fortune, *finally*, after months of sitting in that Podunk real estate office watching Max, his coworker, consume large quantities of onion rings and smoke cigars that smelled like burning rubber. He almost shuddered at the thought. If anything, he was happy as hell to be out of it, happy that he'd learned of the distribution center before anyone else, even happier that he'd been able to convince Major Buchannan of his plan, a plan that smelled a bit but was legal enough to keep them out of jail. And Major, being the greedy man he was, had jumped at it, investing heavily in a tract of affordable housing so that Sweetbriar was the clear choice for those deciding on the warehouse location. He'd taken a chance on Lucas's plan, but it had paid off royally when Lucas convinced the investors to buy one hundred acres of worthless Buchannan land for ten times its worth. Major had shown his appreciation by purchasing a brand new Mercedes Benz for Lucas, and, although Lucas had thanked him, he'd been tempted to tell the man he didn't want a car, he wanted his daughter.

Lucas passed the barber shop and smiled, wondering if Ozzie Burns still gave three-dollar haircuts and if the old geezers in town still played checkers there every Wednesday.

And then he spied the meat-packing plant, and the smile faded from his face as unwelcome memories flooded his mind. He thought of his old man, who'd spent thirty years working in that plant, and of the blue-haired ladies who'd worked beside him, their feet swollen, varicose veins bulging at their knees from years of standing over a conveyor belt. He, too, had spent a fair amount of time in that plant, working summers and weekends. He'd thought his hands and fingers would be permanently stained from handling the bloody, raw meat. In his mind, he could smell the inside of that plant, remember the way that same smell had clung to his hair and clothes. But most of all, he remembered his promise to himself to get out of it. He hadn't wanted to end up like his father, blood-stained T-shirts straining against a hairy pot belly. It was no wonder his mother had left his old man for someone else.

Lucas watched gratefully as the plant disappeared from sight in his rearview mirror. Leaving the town behind, he drove on, passing small farms, until finally he spotted Honey's landscaping business. It was early, not even eight o'clock, and he wondered if she had arrived yet.

Lucas found Honey stacking bales of pine straw behind the building and suspected she was the only one there. Her cheeks were damp, he noted, her face flushed from the already rising heat, and she'd pulled her hair up into a pert ponytail. She had never looked more desirable, wearing denim shorts that emphasized her long legs and a snug tank top that molded nicely to her soft breasts. He'd never forgotten those breasts, with their rose-colored areolas the size of half-dollars, nor had he forgotten how they tasted and felt against his tongue, the nipples as hard as pebbles between his teeth.

"Can we talk?" he asked at last, trying to block the images from his mind and ignore the gentle stirrings of desire that warmed his belly like expensive brandy.

Honey didn't pause in her work. "That depends on what you want to talk about," she said matter-of-factly. "If you're here to talk about landscaping your yard, I'll be happy to listen, but if you're here to badger me—"

"I'm here to find out how soon you can get started on my lot," he interrupted sharply. When she glanced up in surprise, he went on. "Look, Honey, this isn't easy for me either. I should probably have my head examined for having my entire yard dug up just so I could see you again, but the damage is done, and yours is the only landscaping business in town. I just want somebody to repair the damage, okay? You can take it or leave it." He paused, wondering if he'd gone too far. "In the meantime, I'll try to behave myself." There now, he thought. He'd laid all his cards on the table and come as close to an apology as he could. It was up to Honey to reject or accept his offer. He could see by the look on her face that he'd succeeded in putting her on the defensive. It was a tactic he used often in business, a last-ditch effort to pull it all together when it looked as though he might lose the deal. It had worked more times than he could remember.

Honey raised herself up from her work and dusted her hands. "Okay, then," she said. "I think I'd rather leave it."

Lucas felt his mouth drop open. "You would?" His tactic obviously wasn't working with her, he would have to try something else. "But why would you do that when you stand to make good money on the deal? That's just not good business sense, Honey."

"Maybe not. But I'm not going to tolerate this kind of behavior from you, Lucas. You're not going to simply waltz into my life and my place of business and tell me how it's going to be. Besides, there's no excuse for rudeness."

"Was I being rude?" When she didn't answer, he sighed and raked his fingers through his hair. He'd done it again, he thought, started out on the wrong foot with her. Every time he opened his mouth, he drove a wedge deeper between them. He shook his head, his frustration mounting. "What can I do to resolve these problems between us, Honey?" he said at last. When she didn't respond, he added, "If we can't resolve our personal problems at the moment, at least give me a clue how we can settle the problems with my yard."

"You can begin by being polite, Lucas. Surely you haven't forgotten your manners. My other customers don't seem to have a problem with that one simple request."

Lucas couldn't help the grin that broke out on his face. He felt as though he'd just had his hand smacked with a ruler. "I can be nice to you, Honey," he said, his voice dropping an octave so that his meaning was clear.

Honey chose to ignore the remark, despite the prickling sensation along the back of her neck brought on by the husky timbre of his voice. The man really was a rogue, she thought, barreling into her life after all these years, trying to order her around as though he had every right. How it could amuse and irritate her at the same time was a paradox. Perhaps it was because his actions were so typical of him. How like Lucas to go and have his entire yard bulldozed if it served his purpose. But then Lucas was a man of extremes and always had been. The first time she'd gone to dinner with him was after he'd handed her a ten-thousand-dollar check for a charity she'd been heading up. Were there no limits to what he would do to get what he wanted?

"I'm having a difficult time with this, Lucas," she said after a moment. "I never know what to expect from you, and I'm not sure . . . I'm just not sure what you really want from me."

It was on the tip of his tongue to tell her what he wanted, but he knew better. Besides, he'd made it all clear the day before, and she had rejected him flatly. He'd spent a bitter afternoon eating antacids and planning his next move. "I just want you to get my yard in shape before the kids get back," he said. "I know that's asking a lot in a week's time, but"—he shrugged—"I want them to have a nice place to visit, I guess."

She was touched that he was so concerned about their children. Touched, but at the same time wary. "I can't get anyone out there right away to lay sod, Lucas. Eric is working on another project."

"Yes, but you can at least get the place graded and fertilized and help me with trees and shrubs, can't you?"

"I suppose so, but—"

"I don't have a whole lot of time to waste, Honey. I don't think I have to remind you that Todd and Melissa will be back in eight days. I won't have a place for them to play." When she looked unmoved by his words, he went on. "I would do it myself, but I have to paint the place."

"You're doing your own painting?"

He nodded, knowing she would be impressed, which was exactly why he was doing it—that, and because he had nothing else to do. Perhaps she would view him in a different light, see him as being somewhat domesticated. He had to start someplace.

"I've hired some professional painters to do the outside of the house, but they can't start for a few days. I figured I might as well paint the inside. I don't want to furnish the place until the painting is completed." He paused. "I don't suppose you'd be interested in helping me select furniture, would you?"

"Not in the least."

He chuckled. This new Honey wasn't one to mince words. "How about for Todd and Melissa's rooms? I have no idea what they like. And you're good at that kind of stuff. I mean, you did such a great job on our place in Houston."

"Really? You never told me." There was an edge to her voice that told him she would have liked to have known at the time.

"Yeah, well there were a lot of things I never told you but should have." He wished he had told her she had the bluest eyes he'd ever seen and that her hair reminded him of corn silk when the sun hit it just right, but he was about eight years too late. He could regret it all he wanted, but it didn't change things.

"Look, Lucas, I have a business to run. I don't have time to pick out furniture for your house, nor am I going to advise you on the rest of your decorating matters. I'll be more than happy to recommend a decorator to help you, though," she added on a gentler note.

He laughed. "You know, I'm beginning to think you don't like me worth a damn. Is it something you have to work at or does it come naturally?"

Honey could feel the color staining her cheeks. "I don't *dislike* you, Lucas, I simply want to keep our involvement simple and professional."

"And you're afraid if you decorate my house, you'll fall for me again, is that it?"

"Stop teasing me. You know as well as I do how important it is that we develop a good relationship. Our children's happiness and security depend on it."

He looked amused. "I've been trying to have a relationship with you since I hit town," he said matter-of-factly.

"No, Lucas. You've simply been trying to get me into your bed."

He folded his arms across his chest and cocked his head to the side. "Was I that obvious?" he asked, his dark eyes filled with amusement. "And all this time I thought I was the master of subtleness."

"Subtlety has never been one of your virtues."

"Neither has patience, Honey, but I'm learning. I've made it clear how much I want you, but I'm prepared to back off. I'm going to wait until you come to me."

She rolled her eyes heavenward. "Give me a break, Lucas."

"Once you discover for yourself what a changed man I am—how sensitive and caring I can be— you'll do everything in your power to get me back."

He grinned as he said it. He enjoyed sparring with her, exchanging playful banter. It was new and different and strangely exciting. In the past, she'd simply agreed with everything he said. Even he had to admit that could get boring.

"You're wasting my time," she said, and reached for another bale of pine straw.

"You don't even realize how it irks me to see you performing manual labor," he went on. "I would never have permitted it in the past."

"You're certainly right about that."

"But now that I realize how important this is to you, I'd be the last person to object."

"You're all heart, Lucas."

"But you can't blame me for wanting to protect you, can you?"

Honey finished stacking the bales and looked at him. "Protect me from what?"

Her question took him off guard. "Well, from this," he said, indicating the heavy bales of pine straw.

"You wanted to protect me from pine straw?"

"No, I wanted to protect you from . . . harsh things, Honey. I wanted you and the kids to have it easier than I did. I wanted to give you pretty things and see that you had a nice life, that you didn't have to worry about anything. I wanted you to live in a pretty house and wear pretty clothes and—"

"All that sounds mighty archaic, Lucas. Not to mention boring."

"I did it out of love, Honey."

It wasn't his words as much as it was his tone of voice that took Honey by surprise. She nodded. "I know you did. But it almost choked the life right out of me, Lucas."

"I didn't know."

"Because you couldn't."

"I suppose I was a selfish son of a gun, huh?"

Honey knelt to retrieve some pine straw that had escaped the bundles. "I suppose," was all she said.

"Well, now I want to make it up to you."

She shook her head. "No, Lucas. I don't want you to try to make it up to me. I simply want you to live your own life and let me live mine. That's a big house you live in, you know. You should consider remarrying and starting a new family."

Lucas was so taken aback by her words that he couldn't speak. It hurt him more than he could imagine, having her suggest he find another woman, and for the first time, he began to suspect she had truly lost all feeling for him. "That wouldn't bother you, Honey?" he asked softly. "You honestly wouldn't mind my crawling into bed every night with another woman?"

"I think it would be good for you."

"You didn't answer my question," he said, feeling his gut tighten at her response. He wanted to grab her and shake her and make her apologize, but he knew it was a childish thought. Instead, he knelt beside her and waited until she looked up. Their gazes met and locked. "Are you trying to tell me it wouldn't bother you if I brought another woman in my house, made love to her every night, and woke up beside her every morning?" When Honey didn't answer right away, he went on. "Because if that's what you're trying to tell me, then you're lying. I think it *would* bother you."

"It might at first," she finally admitted, "but I think there are worse things."

"Such as?"

"Me living in that house with you," she answered simply.

"You've gotten nasty in your old age, Honey. That's the last thing I would have expected from you."

"I wasn't trying to be cruel," she said, noting his pained expression and feeling guilty because of it, "but I'm learning how to get the things I want in life, Lucas. For the first time, I'm learning how to ask for what I want, how to stand up for myself, how to assert myself. If I come off a bit harsh, I'm sorry. But I never knew how to do these things until I met Eric."

Lucas felt his heart sink to his gut. His fists tightened into balls at his side. "Eric? What is he to you, Honey?"

Honey could see that he was upset. "Not that it's any of your business, but he's the best friend I've ever had. He's the first person who ever seemed to care if I had a thought or an opinion or a dream of my own."

"And does this Eric walk on water as well?"

Her look hardened. "I knew you wouldn't understand, but it's not important. This conversation has nothing to do with landscaping your yard."

"Are you in love with him?"

"Of course I love him."

The color drained from Lucas's face. He stood and turned away. He couldn't face her, knowing that another man may have taken what was once his. "Are you going to marry him?"

Honey laughed. "No. But then I have no intention of marrying again. I'm perfectly content with my life the way it is."

Lucas faced her once more, feeling more confident now that he knew she had no marriage plans. If she truly loved her business partner, she would be willing to try again—at least that's what he told himself. "Don't you ever think of growing old with somebody, Honey?" he asked. "I always thought you and I would grow old together, you know. I figured once we raised the children, we could sit back and enjoy each other. I wanted to be financially stable so neither of us would have to worry about money. I thought we would travel and do things together. Life is so uncertain and unpredictable, but I thought I could count on us being together. I thought I could count on you being there for me."

"Why should I want to grow old with a stranger, Lucas?" Honey asked. "Because that's what we were. You were so interested in making a success of yourself, you didn't see I needed you then. Your children needed you. We can't put our lives on hold until it's convenient for you."

"It wasn't all bad," he said. "I remember good times between us. I remember slipping into bed beside you at night and holding you until you fell asleep. And I remember waking you in the middle of the night and making love to you with the moon shining in through the bedroom window and—"

"Lucas—"

"—and waking up beside you in the morning, your face all flushed and your body still warm from sleep."

"I remember that too, Lucas," she said matter-of-factly. "But the version I remember is the one where you always rushed out of bed as though the devil himself were after you, because you had an appointment you couldn't break. You never had time to simply lie there with me and enjoy it. I thought that's what growing old with somebody meant, capturing those special moments in between."

"I had to make a living, Honey. We had bills coming out our ears."

"Yes, we did, didn't we? But it never occurred to you that we didn't need that big house and a Cadillac and Mercedes in the driveway and everything else that came with it. It never occurred to you that we didn't need a fifty-thousand-dollar boat we seldom used. And it never occurred to you that I could work and take some of the pressure off you."

"It occurred to me," he said tightly.

"Yet it didn't stop you. It didn't prevent you from going to extremes where our children were concerned as well." She shook her head. "Todd and Melissa had enough toys to stock a children's store," she said. "I used to feel so guilty at Christmas and birthdays because you bought so much. It was almost shameful. They were the only kids I knew who had three of everything."

"I wanted them to have more than I did when I was growing up."

"Of course you did. But they had more than they ever could hope to play with."

He shrugged. "Well, you ended up giving most of their toys away to charity," he said.

"Yes, because I wanted them to appreciate what they got, maybe even earn some of their things by doing chores the way most kids do. I didn't want servants cleaning their rooms when they were supposed to be learning to do it themselves. I didn't want things handed to them on silver platters, Lucas. Because life, like you said, is unpredictable, and our children may not always have someone to pick up after them and cook for them and buy them pretty things." She had to stop to catch her breath. "Todd and Melissa need to know that everything has a price."

"Okay, so I went overboard," he said, sitting down on a bale of pine straw. "You have no idea what it's like to want for things and know you can't have them," he said after a moment. "You have no idea what it's like to know . . ." He hesitated. "To know you don't measure up in other people's eyes." He looked at her. "I wanted to measure up, Honey. Maybe I went about it the wrong way, but I didn't know how else to do it."

Honey sighed heavily and took a seat beside him. Finally, she spoke. "I'm glad you told me this, Lucas," she said, "because it helps me understand why you were so . . . driven. I realize now that you weren't purposefully neglecting us."

"Neglecting you?" he said in disbelief.

She nodded. "I thought the children and I were just another one of your possessions, like the house and cars. I see now that you had our best interests at heart."

"I never even suspected you felt that way. It's my own fault for not telling you how I felt, telling you how important you were in my life." He paused, feeling very sad about the whole thing. "Can you ever forgive me?" He searched her face.

Honey felt her throat clog with emotion, but she

met his gaze. "Yes, I can forgive you, Lucas. Of course I can."

"Can you ever love me again, Honey?"

She stiffened, knowing in her heart she'd seen it coming. "Lucas, I will always feel deeply toward you. You were my first love, my husband for five years, the father of my children."

He shook his head. "That's not good enough, Honey. I want more. I want the kind of love from you that most people only dream about. I want to be so close to you that you don't know where you leave off and I begin."

She smiled softly to ease what she was about to say. "You're asking for more than I'm willing to give."

"Maybe for now I am." He stood and shoved his hands into his pockets, knowing he had to put some distance between them or he would take her in his arms and kiss her. "But like I said. I can be patient if I have to."

Honey knew Lucas had every intention of getting her back, and knowing what a shrewd operator he was, knowing that he would go to any extreme to have her—including leaving a prosperous company and moving across the state to be near her—frightened her. She wasn't sure she was emotionally equipped to deal with him. She had made a mistake by agreeing to work with him. If she was smart, she would hand the job over to Eric and get on with something else. But Eric was tied up with another job, and Lucas had made it clear he was in a hurry. Her heart pounded in her chest as she felt Lucas's gaze on her, caressing her face as surely as if he'd reached out and stroked her with his fingertips.

She had promised herself she was finished running from him, convinced herself she was ready to face him and the feelings that always surfaced as a result. But she knew in her heart that if ever there was a time to run, it was now.

Four

Honey began the work on Lucas's lot the following morning, arriving at his house with a large rotary tiller in the back of her truck. When he questioned her about it, she was quick to explain.

"That earth monster you ordered in to tear up your yard packed the soil too tightly," she said. "We'll have to break it up before we can add nutrients or plant sod." She started to walk away.

"What's the shovel for?" he asked, when she pulled it from her truck.

"I'm going to dig a hole."

"How come?"

Honey sighed. "I want to take a closer look at your soil."

"Why?"

She rolled her eyes heavenward. "To make sure you don't have a drainage problem. Lucas, you promised to stay out of my way so I could do my job and—"

"All right," he said, holding up his hands as

though surrendering. "Would you like a cup of coffee before you get started."

"No, you've already given me two cups. Now, if you don't mind—"

"Are you going to do all this work by yourself?"

She shook her head. "I have a man coming later to operate the tiller. But I have things to do before he gets here."

"A man?"

Honey could feel her exasperation mounting. "I hired someone from a temporary agency to help out. Now, please, Lucas." She pointed toward the house. "Go."

"I'm going, I'm going," he grumbled.

From the corner of her eye, Honey watched Lucas make his way to the house. The jeans he wore were old and faded and splattered with white paint, as was his navy T-shirt. Both fit his lean body snugly, emphasizing the masculine lines and taut muscles. Just looking at him, those trim hips and waist, the wide shoulders, made her mouth go dry. She had seen him in the shower enough times to know what he looked like without clothes, lean and brown and feathered with dark hair from head to toe. The thought made her blush.

Honey had not known a man intimately before she had met Lucas; in fact, she'd been a virgin. Of course, she'd had urges like everybody else, but she had been terrified of sex. Major had seen to that, telling her stories of young girls who'd ruined their lives with disease and unwanted pregnancy and emotional problems due to premarital sex, long before she'd even known what the word meant. A man would never respect a woman who lay with him without the benefit of marriage,

Major had told her many times, and Honey decided at a young age that she wasn't willing to take such risks for just a few minutes of gratification.

Her virginity had been a subject close to Major's heart, she learned, and one he'd championed from the moment her breasts began to develop at age eleven. Major, who by nature had a queasy stomach, could not discuss things like operations at the supper table, but her virginity was wide open for discussion.

"I will not have folks in this town thinking I've raised a tramp," he said more times than she could remember. Not that there was any possibility of her practicing any of the carnal pleasures Major so often warned her about. She was not permitted to do the things that most young people enjoyed, and when Major *did* allow an outing, Vera acted as chaperone. When it came time for college, Honey was sent to a religious girl's school that catered to wealthy families and saw to it the girls remained "ladies." They did not have the opportunity to be tempted by the opposite sex, except on rare occasions when they were allowed to attend dances— but only under strict observation. And then in her junior year, a classmate of Honey's became pregnant somehow and arranged for an abortion. Complications set in and the girl almost died. Not only did it scandalize the school and her family, but Honey later learned the girl would never be able to bear children as a result. Honey could not imagine going to Major with such a problem. However, there were times she found herself thinking about sex more than she thought a decent girl should. Major had warned her of perverts, those who could not free their minds of sexual thoughts, and Honey feared she was suffering that very malaise.

When she'd met Lucas, a raw-boned and virile man, Honey had known she wanted him. She found him sitting in her father's private office one day, exuding such masculinity that she could barely breathe, and she'd known she had to have him. He was so different from the pimply-faced boys she'd known who stuttered and stammered and tripped over their own feet when she was near. Lucas was not a boy at all. He was all man, strong and self-assured and the best looking thing she'd ever laid eyes on. And Major must have suspected her feelings, because he had been hell-bent on keeping them apart. It was one time he hadn't succeeded.

Honey shook her head and grabbed her shovel, trying to concentrate on the task at hand. She dug with a vengeance, throwing her whole body into her work as she tried to block further thoughts of Lucas. She would not think about the past or play that "what if" game she was so famous for. She knew the game well, had it down to an art. *What if* things had been different and Lucas had given a little more of himself to his family instead of being so consumed with his success? *What if* she had demanded he spend more time with them, take the time to get to know his son and daughter? *What if* she had put her foot down and told him she was going to find a part-time job and start making some of her own decisions? *What if* she had refused to entertain clients every weekend and found friends of her own?

Honey shoved the thoughts from her mind once again, knowing how futile they were. She had tried to get what she wanted from Lucas during their marriage in her own feeble way. She had tried to draw him closer to her and the children, but he'd been too busy to see how desperately they needed him. And she had tried to make him understand how important it was for her to have something of her own, something she could be proud of. Lucas had suggested she take a ceramics class. He couldn't see how important it was to her, she knew, because he was incapable of seeing outside himself. He couldn't see that his children needed him, because he was so absorbed with his own needs. And Honey had decided it would be easier to dissolve the marriage than live with constant loneliness and frustration. Besides, she wasn't really giving up much. Lucas had never belonged to her.

When Lucas stepped out on his front porch twenty minutes later holding two tall glasses of lemonade, he saw Honey leaning over the back of her truck looking for something. He hurried across the yard, his gaze on the frosty glasses, trying to prevent them from spilling. "How about something cold to drink?" he called out.

Honey glanced up at him and sighed. Was there no getting rid of the man? she wondered. Wasn't it bad enough she had to think of him all the time? Why must she be forced to see him every waking minute of her day? Then she saw he was headed straight for the gaping three-foot-deep hole she'd just dug and forgot everything else. "Lucas, watch out!" she cried.

She was a split second too late.

Surprise filtered across Lucas's face as he put his left foot down and found nothing. His foot landed in the hole with enough force to jar his whole body, and the glasses were lost. They shattered on the ground nearby, spilling the freshly squeezed lemonade he'd worked so hard to prepare. With his foot lodged in the hole, he fell face first in the dirt.

"Lucas!" Honey dropped what she was holding and ran.

Lucas pushed himself up on his elbows, sputtering and cussing and spitting dirt. "What the hell!" he demanded, glancing around at his leg, which was buried almost to his knee.

"Oh, Lucas, I'm so sorry! I tried to warn you." Honey dusted the dirt from his face and eyes as she anxiously assessed the rest of him. "Here, let me help you up." He let out a loud groan when she tried to pull him free. "Oh, no! You don't think your foot is broken, do you?"

Lucas shook his head. "No, it hurts too much to be broken." He spit more dirt.

"Come on," she coaxed, trying to wrap one of his arms around her shoulders. "Try to stand."

Lucas was genuinely touched by her concern. It occurred to him suddenly that Honey felt responsible for his accident; otherwise she wouldn't be hovering over him as though expecting the great angel of death to snatch him up right there on the spot. He almost smiled at the thought, and in his heart he knew he had no choice but to play it for all it was worth. His look turned grim. "I think maybe I *did* break it, Honey," he said, tightening his jaw as he spoke.

"Oh, Lucas!" Honey's eyes widened in alarm. "This is all my fault," she said, helping him to his feet after much effort. "Here, lean against me so I can have a look." Doing as she said, Lucas balanced himself on his right foot, reveling in her softness as she leaned forward to examine the other. She pulled off his sneaker and sock and ran trembling fingers along his ankle. "Does this hurt?"

"Like a son of a gun," he said, each gentle squeeze of her hand sending currents of heat up his calf and thigh. He closed his eyes and gritted his teeth, memorizing the feel of her hands on his body. He had ached for her touch for so long that it was almost more than he could stand.

"Oh, Lucas, you really are hurt," Honey said, seeing the pained expression on his face. "I have to get you to a doctor."

His eyes popped open. "Doctor?"

"Yes. You'll need this X-rayed immediately."

"No!"

Honey snapped her head up at his tone of voice. "No?"

"Uh, I don't have a family doctor," he said quickly. "You know, being new in town and all." He was grasping for excuses.

"I'll take you to my doctor."

"And I'll have to wait all day to see him."

"Not for an emergency."

"Anyway, I don't think it's really broken," Lucas said, amending his previous diagnosis. "Look, I can put weight on it." He touched his foot tentatively to the ground. "I wouldn't be able to do that if it was broken."

"Lucas, you *have* to go to the doctor," she insisted. "You may have torn a ligament."

He couldn't help but feel a twinge of guilt at the anxious look on her face. "Why don't you help me inside the house?" he suggested. "Let me get cleaned up first, then if it still hurts, I'll go. Deal?"

"Okay," she said begrudgingly, remembering suddenly how much Lucas hated going to the doctor. She had sent him off to work a couple of times during their marriage with the flu and looking so sick, she'd thought he'd die. He'd insisted on nursing it himself. Instead of arguing further, though, she anchored his arm over her shoulder and helped him toward the house. "I don't understand you, Lucas," she mumbled as she helped him up the front steps. "You're as bad as Todd and Melissa when it comes to seeing a doctor."

He chuckled, enjoying her closeness and the way her hair fell over his arm. It was thick and clean and smelled of flowers. "I guess we're big chickens when it comes down to it."

Honey looked up at him. "I can't imagine you being afraid of anything, Lucas." They paused at the top of the steps, each of them breathing hard from exertion. Their gazes met and locked.

"You'd be surprised, Honey," he said. "I get scared like everybody else. I've just learned to hide it better than most."

Honey wanted to question him further, to ask what he could possibly be afraid of, but she didn't. For one thing, it was just too personal to discuss, and she had decided to steer clear of anything personal when it came to Lucas. Instead, she pushed open his front door and helped him inside.

"Where to?" she asked once they'd stepped into the living room. "Would you like to lie down?"

"I want to wash up first," he said. "I feel as if I've

got dirt in my eyes. Somehow it even managed to get inside my T-shirt."

"Oh, Lucas, I feel so badly about this."

"It was an accident, stop worrying."

She helped him to the bathroom but stood at a respectful distance as he hobbled to the old-fashioned pedestal sink. "Can I get you something?" she offered, feeling suddenly shy with him.

"How about a clean towel?" he said, motioning toward a cabinet beside the door. Honey nodded, reached inside the linen cabinet, and pulled out a fluffy towel, which had the price sticker attached. She pulled off the tag and turned to Lucas, just as he reached for the hem of his T-shirt and peeled it off. Honey stood there, mouth agape, and watched.

Lucas turned on the faucets, scooped water into his big hands, and bathed his face and chest, then splashed water on the back of his neck, which was gritty with dirt. Finally, he stuck his entire head beneath the stream of water, working his fingers against his scalp. His muscles rippled with the effort. Honey followed every move with her eyes. Yes, his back and shoulders were still as broad as she remembered, she thought, tapering into a trim waist and lean hips. When he turned and reached for the towel, she was waiting. She handed it to him, blinking furiously to avoid eye contact.

"Thanks," he said, grabbing the towel from her. He dried his head briskly, then ran the towel lightly across his chest and the back of his neck, noting with satisfaction the way she watched him from beneath those gold lashes of hers. No, she was not immune to him, as she would have him believe, he thought. He draped the towel over a rack and faced her. Honey automatically reached for the doorknob, wanting to escape the bathroom, which had suddenly shrunk in size. Unfortunately, she knew she was going to have to assist him.

"How does it feel?" she asked, indicating his foot with a nod of her head.

"Sore."

"It looks puffy. Does it look puffy to you?"

He glanced at his foot and thought it looked much the same. "Maybe a little."

"You need to put ice on it. Do you have an ice pack?" When he shook his head, she went on. "It doesn't matter, I can make one."

"I really hate to put you to the trouble."

"Don't be silly. Here, let me help you into the living room so you can sit." She hesitated a second, trying to prepare herself mentally, knowing that he would have to touch her again. She stepped closer.

Draping one arm over her shoulder, Lucas hobbled into the living room and sank onto the couch, almost pulling her down with him. He felt her go stiff in his arms. "Sorry," he said as she tried to wriggle free.

Honey's knees were trembling. His nearness, the smell of his flesh, the feel of his damp hair brushing against her arm were more than she could bear. "Uh, that's okay." Her voice didn't sound like her own. "Just sit tight. I'll be back in a jiffy." She hurried away.

When Honey reached the kitchen, she was literally gasping. She paused at the sink to catch her breath, feeling as though her lungs had suddenly grown too small. She gripped the counter tightly and closed her eyes, intent on getting herself under control. Why had she ever thought herself over Lucas McKay? she wondered. She was as attracted to him as she had been the first time she'd seen him. Nothing had changed. Only now, after having lived with him for five years, she knew where these feelings could lead, knew exactly what it would take to quell the persistent yearnings he evoked in her every time he looked at her. And she knew Lucas would only be too happy to accommodate her. She knew it from the way he watched her, the way he spoke her name. He was simply biding his time, waiting for her to make the first move. And there was not a damn thing she could do about it, she told herself. She couldn't very well leave him lying on the sofa with a bum foot, especially since she'd caused the accident herself. Somehow, she would have to detach herself emotionally from the potent messages he was sending her. It wouldn't be easy, but she couldn't risk giving him anything of herself. He would ultimately take it all.

When Honey returned to the living room a few minutes later carrying a homemade ice pack, Lucas was reclining on the sofa with his sore foot propped on the arm rest. "It's going to be cold," she warned, indicating the ice pack. Then, very carefully, she placed it on the uppermost part of his foot. Much to her dismay, it would not stay. She tried several times, then finally held it there, aware that his gaze never left her.

"Sit down," Lucas said after another minute had passed and it looked as though she had no intention of doing so. He slid his long legs toward the back of the couch so she had room. Honey sat down stiffly and focused all her attention on his foot. The scene was much too intimate for her liking, and she was uncomfortably aware that he was bare chested. There was no way of looking at his face without seeing that chest, without noticing the firm muscles and crisp chest hair. But how could she suggest he put on a shirt? No, she didn't like it one bit, she thought, and she was careful not to touch his foot with her fingers. Skin touching skin was dangerous. She gripped the ice pack as if it were a lifeline.

Lucas could not help but notice Honey's discomfort, and it pleased him. Her back was ramrod straight, as though she were afraid to relax and risk brushing against his jean-clad calf. In the quietness of the room he gazed at her, watching the unsteady rise and fall of her chest. She was breathing too fast and fussing unnecessarily with her hair as though irritated with it. She was as anxious as a treed kitten, he told himself, and that thought sent a tremor of satisfaction through his body. She may not love him, but she was sure as hell aware of him. For the moment it was enough.

"Are you in pain?" Honey asked, desperate to break the silence that had sprang up between them. Her gaze met his hesitantly.

He was in pain, Lucas thought, but it had nothing to do with his foot. "A little. No big deal."

"I think we should wrap it in an Ace bandage or something."

His thoughts outraced hers. That meant she'd have to touch him again. "Yeah, that might be a good idea."

She sighed. "Maybe you should come home with me."

It was all he could do to keep from falling off the couch. "Come home with you?" he repeated dumbly.

She nodded grimly. "Well, it's obvious you're going to have to stay off of your foot," she said. "At least for a day or so. If you come to my place, you can take it easy. You won't have to worry about painting or cooking for yourself. Anyway, I'd feel a lot less guilty." It wasn't only guilt, she knew. She felt safer in her own home, knowing that Vera was nearby. If he stayed where he was, she would be forced to check on him constantly, perhaps even care for him, and that would mean spending more time alone with him. Him coming home with her seemed less . . . dangerous. "I have a first aid kit at home," she added. "I'm sure I can find something to wrap it with. Unless you want me to take you to the doctor, after all."

"No, I don't think I need a doctor," he said, trying to catch a glance at his foot from over her shoulder. "I just need to give it some rest, as you said."

"Then you'll come home with me? At least for tonight? I can bring you back in the morning."

Lucas forced himself to remain calm and not pounce on the suggestion like a hound dog on a soup bone. But it was all he could do to keep his excitement from showing. "Aw, I hate to be a burden to you, Honey," he said, trying to affect a solemn tone.

"You won't be," she assured him. "You can spend the day resting and watching videos if you like. Or maybe lie out by the pool, if you promise to stay off your foot."

It sounded too good to be true, and Lucas wondered if maybe his luck was beginning to change.

"Well, if you're sure you don't mind. I'll need to pack a few things."

"I'll do it," she offered, thankful to have a reason to escape. "Just tell me what you'll need."

Lucas told her, and she hurried into his bedroom to collect his things. "Don't forget to pack my bathing suit," he called out. "It should be in the bottom drawer of that old dresser. And don't forget my underwear." He smiled to himself, wondering if Honey still owned that strapless teal blue bathing suit that made his eyes sparkle like Christmas lights.

In the next room, Honey fumbled in the top drawer of a battered dresser for socks and underwear, wishing now she had let him do it. There was absolutely nothing more intimate than handling a man's underwear, she decided, feeling a hot flush stain her cheeks. She gathered the clothes up and slammed the drawer harder than she meant to.

"Is everything okay in there?" Lucas called out.

"F-fine," she sputtered. "Do you have an overnight bag or something I can put your clothes in?"

Lucas grinned. He'd bet his last dime she'd gotten flustered going through his underwear drawer. "There's a small suitcase in the closet. Are you sure you don't need my help?"

"I can do it," she said tersely. "Do you care which shirts and slacks I pack?"

"Naw, you can pick them out. You always had good taste."

Honey gritted her teeth and strode purposefully to the closet. Inside she found his suitcases, grabbed the smallest, and flung it on the bed, where the tousled sheets seemed to stare back at her as blatantly as his underwear had a moment before. She finished packing in record time, deciding it was better just to get the job done than to lament over which outfits he might want and try to decide which shirt would look best against his dark coloring and . . . Honey slammed the suitcase closed and snapped the locks.

"Ready?" she asked, standing before him a moment later, trying her best to appear cool and composed. "Oh, you'll need another shirt," she said, noting he was still bare chested. How could she have forgotten? She turned back toward the bedroom.

"And my toothbrush," he reminded her, trying to keep the smile from his voice. Oh yes, life was beginning to look good again, he thought.

Honey returned with his toothbrush and a clean shirt. "I trust you can put this on by yourself," she said, dropping it onto his lap.

"If I have to." His mouth twitched at the corners.

Honey didn't respond. With things as tense as they were, the two of them certainly didn't need to swap sexual banter. She helped him out the front door, carrying his suitcase in her free hand.

They covered the miles to Honey's in record time, and Lucas, gripping the door handle as they bounced over the country roads in her truck, couldn't help but wonder why she was in such a hurry. He convinced himself it was because she couldn't wait to spend some quality time with him. But when they arrived at the Buchannan mansion, his hopes were quickly dashed. Vera met them at the front door wearing a scowl that would have rivaled a storm cloud.

"What's this?" she asked, drawing herself up as Honey helped Lucas through the doorway.

"Lucas hurt himself," Honey said, "and since he refuses to go to the doctor, I suggested he spend a day or two here."

"Here?" Vera asked in obvious alarm. Her gaze met Lucas's over Honey's shoulder, and he grinned. The woman snapped her eyes away with a force that would have made anyone else dizzy. "Why here?"

"Because it's my fault he had the accident," Honey said, closing the door behind them and setting Lucas's suitcase down. "I don't have time to explain," she said hurriedly. "I have to leave."

"Leave?" Lucas and Vera chimed in unison.

Lucas stepped forward without thinking to hobble. Vera, he saw, didn't miss it with those buzzard eyes of hers. "Where are you going?"

"I have to go back to your place," she said. "I have someone coming to till your lot, remember?" She turned her attention back to Vera. "He needs an ice pack for his foot. Once the swelling goes down, you'll have to wrap it. You know where the first aid kit is."

Vera was so shocked by the request that she didn't answer right away, though her face grew red. "You want *me* to do it?" Vera finally asked in a tone that suggested she'd just as soon shovel cow manure from the pasture.

"Please, Vera, if you don't mind," Honey said. "I can't waste any more time. And Lucas—" She paused and gave him a stern look. "Please stay off that foot. It isn't going to get any better unless you do. Now I have to go." She was out the door before either of them could protest.

Five

Vera didn't speak right away. Instead, she gazed at Lucas's sock-covered foot. Lucas heard Honey's truck start up out front and a second later pull out of the gravel driveway. He wondered what in the world he'd ever done to deserve such a horrible twist of fate.

"What's going on here, Lucas McKay?" Vera demanded.

Lucas hesitated. He might fool Honey about his fake wound, but he would never fool Vera. Honey had been so caught up in guilt and remorse that she hadn't suspected his scheme. Vera would. He had a choice. He could try to keep the charade going and maybe even make Vera madder, or he could come clean and get booted out on his behind. "I hurt my foot," he said innocently, deciding to try his first choice.

Vera sniffed. "Try again."

Lucas folded his arms across his chest and leaned against the wall. Plan number one had obviously failed. He could feel the gravel on his fanny. "You're too quick for me, Vera," he said, chuckling. He dropped the smile. "I'm trying to get my wife and kids back, okay?" He held his hands out as though surrendering. "So far nothing has worked. This is sort of a last-ditch effort. So the rest is up to you. You can either help me, or you can get in the car and drive to my place and tell Honey it's a scam."

Vera didn't budge. "Why should I want to help you?"

Lucas unfolded his arms and stepped closer. "Because I worship the ground that girl walks on, and you know it." He pointed at her as he spoke. "And because I'm the father of her children. There's nothing I wouldn't do for the three of them."

"Get your finger out of my face before I bite it off and spit it at you," Vera said. Lucas pulled his finger away quickly and tucked his hand in his pocket, where it was safe. "Now you listen to me, Lucas McKay," she said, stepping so close, Lucas could smell her perfume, which was sweet as vanilla extract. "You don't come into this house and tell me how I'm gonna do things. When Honey was living with you as your wife, you didn't treat her any better than three-day-old bread. What makes you think I'd allow such a thing to happen again?"

He didn't hesitate. "Because you know in your heart that I love Honey as much as you do," he said simply. "And because I believe you're a fair person. People make mistakes. Heaven knows I've made mine. But I've paid for those mistakes, Vera, believe me." After a moment, he went on. "And because you have no right to judge me. If Honey had an unhappy childhood, you were just as much to blame as the man who raised her."

Vera's head snapped up. "I don't know what you're talking about."

"Honey was too little to stand up to Major in the beginning. You could have done something. You *should* have done something. And I never mistreated Honey when she lived with me. If I made all of Honey's decisions for her, it was only because she didn't know how to make them for herself when I met her. And because . . ." He paused. "I guess I enjoyed feeling as though she needed me."

"She doesn't need you now," Vera said smugly.

"Not to make her decisions, maybe, but she needs me just the same. She needs the love I have to offer. Or have you convinced her otherwise?"

"I haven't convinced her of nothing," Vera answered. "I don't tell Honey how to live her life. And you're wrong about my not trying to defend her as a young'un," she added, her face growing red once more. "I stood up to that old buzzard Major Buchannan many times. I even got fired for doing it, then had to beg for my job back. I learned to keep my mouth shut, because without me, Honey would have been all alone in this world. I tried to give her the love her mother couldn't and the love her father wouldn't. So don't you dare come in here and accuse me of—" Vera had to stop to catch her breath. She was literally gasping, so badly, in fact, it caught Lucas's attention.

"What's wrong?" he asked, stepping closer.

"You've upset me, fool, what do you think is wrong?" Vera stumbled toward a bench along the wall and sank onto it heavily.

Lucas frowned. "Are you sick?"

"I'm seventy years old, of course I'm sick!"

"I'm sorry I upset you. Can I get you something?"

"I'll be okay after a bit," she said, growing calmer. "I'm just getting old."

"Which is why you should welcome me back in Honey's life," Lucas said gently. "I'll see that she and the children never want for anything. Will you help me?"

Vera studied him for a long while. "No, I won't help you, Lucas McKay," she said at last. "If you want to win Honey back, you'll have to do it on your own. But I won't give you away about your foot, if that's what you mean. Now come on in the kitchen, and I'll wrap it in a bandage." She got up and Lucas started to follow. She paused suddenly and looked at him. "I hope you don't make the same mistake you made with her in the past, boy," she said firmly. "If you do, I'll come down hard, so hard on you, you won't know what hit you."

When Honey arrived home that evening, hot and tired, she found Lucas sprawled on the sofa watching television, his foot wrapped in a bandage. "How's it feel?" she asked.

Lucas was so glad to see her, it was all he could do to keep from jumping up and running to her. "Better, I suppose," he said lamely. Vera entered the room carrying a pitcher of iced tea and two glasses.

"Oh, Vera, just what I needed," Honey said, falling into an overstuffed chair. She waited for Vera to fill one of the glasses and accepted it gratefully.

"I'll take one of those if you don't mind," Lucas said, and was awarded with a dark look from the older woman.

Honey didn't miss the exchange. She smiled. "Well, I see you two are getting along okay. Vera, what did you think of Lucas's foot?"

Vera sat the tray down on the coffee table. "It doesn't look good," she said, not quite making eye contact.

Honey arched one graceful brow in surprise. "Really? It's nothing serious, is it?"

"Well—" Vera glanced at Lucas, then busied herself pouring his tea. "He's going to have to stay off of it for a few days. Otherwise, I'm afraid it'll get worse."

"A few days?" Honey said. "But I thought it was a simple sprain."

"It got worse after you left," Lucas pitched in. "Real nasty looking, if I do say so myself."

Honey was genuinely concerned. "I'm sorry, Lucas. I had no idea. Are you in pain?"

"Yeah, but I'll be okay," he said bravely.

"Vera, why don't you fix Lucas one of those drinks you used to make Daddy when his rheumatism acted up. You know, those hot toddies?"

"In this heat?" Vera asked.

"Oh, it's not hot inside. Besides, it's the least we can do, since I'm the one responsible for Lucas's accident. You don't mind, do you?"

Vera glanced in Lucas's direction and sniffed. He grinned. "No, I don't mind," she said begrudgingly, even though her look said otherwise. She left the room, sniffing as she made her way down the hall and toward the kitchen.

Honey smiled at Lucas and took a sip of her iced

tea. "Once you drink one of Vera's toddies, you won't know the meaning of pain," she said laughingly. She glanced at her wristwatch. "Well, I think I'll jump in the shower before dinner. Did I mention that Eric will be joining us tonight?"

Lucas, taking a long sip of his iced tea, almost choked. "Eric?" he sputtered.

Honey nodded. "When I told him of your accident and that I had invited you here, he insisted on stopping by to meet you. So I told him to stay for dinner. He should be here any minute. I'd better get moving." She stood and made her way to the door just as Vera entered carrying a tall, steaming mug.

"Here's your drink," she told Lucas, and set it on the coffee table in front of him with a loud thunk. "Enjoy it," she added through clenched teeth.

Honey didn't seem to notice Vera's animosity. "I have to take a shower, Vera," she said quickly. "Eric is joining us for dinner tonight. You don't mind, do you?" When the woman shook her head, Honey went on. "And would you please prop a pillow beneath Lucas's foot, he looks terribly uncomfortable."

"Uh-huh," was all Vera said.

"And try to find the remote control device, please. I don't want him walking back and forth to change channels." Honey looked at Lucas. "You can plan on staying here for the next few days until that foot gets better. Vera will keep you company." She didn't see the look the woman shot him as she left the room.

Honey stepped into the warm spray of water and sighed her immense pleasure as the steam rose and swathed her naked body like a sensual cloud.

With her eyes closed, she reached blindly for the bottle of baby shampoo and poured a liberal amount into her thick hair, then worked it into a rich lather. The smell of the shampoo made her think of her children, and she smiled.

Darn, but she missed them. She was mentally counting down the days until their return. She often wanted to get in her truck and drive to the camp to see them, but she knew Todd would never forgive her. Over and over again, she had told herself they were too young, especially Melissa, to be away for two whole weeks. The fact that other parents let their children go for that length of time didn't make it any easier. But she had forced herself to let them go, simply because she knew it was best. She would not allow herself to smother them as she'd been smothered by Major. Somehow she would get through the next week, she told herself. She would continue to send postcards and treats, but she would not disrupt this time for them. Besides, she had her hands full at the moment with Lucas. She did not want to put Todd and Melissa through the same turmoil. They had been through enough.

Honey rinsed her hair clean and began soaping her body, but her thoughts were centered on the man downstairs, who'd come back into her life and turned her emotions topsy-turvy. She should have her head examined for inviting him into her house, she thought. It had seemed a good idea at the time, but now it looked as though she would be forced to endure his presence longer than she'd planned. How would she be able to sit across the dinner table from him without thinking of the past, without remembering the good times they'd shared? And there had been good times. That's why leaving had been so difficult.

Honey blinked back sudden tears. She had spent the better part of the day trying not to cry, trying instead to concentrate on the work she had to do on Lucas's lot. Instead, she'd found herself thinking of him, of their first time together, when he'd presented her with that check and an invitation to dinner.

She had slept with him that night. She always burned with shame at the thought, and it was not something she would ever share with her daughter, but at the time it had seemed so right that they should end the evening in each other's arms. She had been the one to suggest going to his place, amidst bouts of blushing, and she remembered how he'd arched one dark brow in surprise at the open invitation but accepted nevertheless. It was the only time she remembered catching him off guard, since Lucas prided himself on his self-control.

Honey knew in her heart that if she had it to do over, she would make the same decision. Lucas had been kind and patient with her as a lover, kissing and cuddling her against him until she'd felt secure. He'd undressed her slowly, pressing his lips against each spot he'd bared and complimenting her loveliness so sincerely that by the time she'd been completely naked before him, she'd felt truly beautiful. He'd kissed her all over, her throat and breasts, her thighs and stomach, and finally he'd buried his face against the tuft of gold between her thighs. And when she'd climaxed against him, she'd known Major had lied to her about the things that went on between men and women. She had not felt dirty and soiled, she'd felt as though heaven had opened a small window for her to peer through. And for the first time in her life she'd felt worthy of love, love that she'd been denied by her own parents. There had been no pain when Lucas had entered her, only pleasure, and the sounds of their sighs floating to the ceiling. Afterward, he'd bathed her face and the sore area between her legs with a cool cloth, his gaze tender and loving. And when she'd nestled against his solid chest and felt the steady pounding of her heart, she'd known she loved him, loved him with the same fierceness and intensity that great poets wrote about. She had never felt happier.

That happiness abated somewhat, however, when she arrived home in the wee hours of the morning, her lips swollen from Lucas's kisses, her hair tousled about her head beguilingly, to find Major waiting, filled with a rage she had never before seen. Honey cringed at the memory. But Lucas had been there for her, standing up to the man she'd always feared and sometimes even hated.

"Don't you dare lay a hand on her," he'd warned Major, shielding her with his own body. "She is going to be my wife." Honey was so proud of him for standing up to Major that it didn't occur to her that Lucas had never officially proposed. Then he'd cocked his head to the side and smiled. "With any kind of luck, she's already carrying your grandchild."

Honey thought Major would surely have a stroke at the news, and she had never seen him fight so desperately for control. His eyes bulged, and his face turned fire-engine red. "Take her, then," he'd said. "Nobody else is going to want her now that she's been with a simple meat packer's son."

Honey left that night with only the clothes on her back and Lucas's promise to select an entire new wardrobe for her. He did the very next day, dressing her in the same linen suits and hats she'd worn all her life. And she did not tell him how weary she was of those styles, simply because he found such pleasure in choosing them for her. And, too, she knew it was a matter of pride. "I don't want anyone thinking I can't afford to dress you as well as your father did," Lucas said. She did insist on choosing her own lingerie, however, and the way Lucas's eyes blazed like hot coals when he saw her in them told her she'd made the right choice.

They were married two days later at the courthouse in Sweetbriar with only Lucas's friend Max in attendance. They honeymooned in a coastal town in Mexico in a red-tiled hotel, where they baked in the sun by day and made love long into the night. He had told her one night, just before he'd shuddered in her arms, that she had the face of an angel and the body of a prostitute. She had secretly cried later, because she hadn't understood it was his way of complimenting her. Had he told her she was as graceful as a Texas bluebonnet in the breeze or as pretty as the pink and purple canyons of the Big Bend, she would have understood. But Lucas wasn't one to spout off flowery phrases between the sheets. The words he whispered in her ears during their lovemaking had nothing to do with great literature or love songs, the kinds of things she would have expected to hear from a loving husband. Lucas's words had been bold and a bit raunchy for her tastes, enough to make her blush afterward just thinking about them.

They'd moved to Houston, and Todd had been born almost nine months to the day after their first date.

The water cooled in the shower after a moment, and Honey shivered. Her nipples puckered in response, and she wondered if it was indeed the water causing her body to react so or thoughts of Lucas. But then, Lucas had always had that effect on her, making her hot and flushed and tingly on the outside while inside she felt as soft and warm as freshly churned butter. Her eyes teared once more, and she wondered if Lucas had any idea what she had been going through since he'd hit town. She had tried so hard to act tough and make him think she was over him. Sometimes she even convinced herself. Falling out of love with a man was sort of like having the chicken pox, she once told herself. The fever might disappear, but you still itched from time to time.

She still itched for Lucas McKay.

Honey emerged twenty minutes later dressed in crisp white walking shorts and a cranberry knit top. Because she had run out of time, she wore very little makeup, and her hair was still damp from her shower. Lucas thought she'd never looked prettier, her cheeks flushed the same color as her blouse, her eyes sparkling like jewels. But before he could tell her as much, the doorbell rang, and Honey hurried to answer it.

"Lucas, this is Eric Severnson," she said, escorting the blond giant of a man into the room. Lucas, his foot propped on a pillow, offered his hand, and the younger man pumped it enthusiastically.

"I've been looking forward to meeting you, Lucas," Eric said, his Swedish accent very noticeable. "Honey has told me much about you."

Lucas didn't quite know how to respond, and he was a bit intimidated by the man's size. Being over six feet tall himself, he was not accustomed to looking up to someone, but this golden-haired Adonis topped him by a good six inches. He looked as though he should be pumping iron in some gym, Lucas thought, wondering if Honey had developed a sudden liking for the body-building type. The thought irritated him, and he shoved it aside. The man was probably hooked on steroids.

"Nice to meet you," Lucas said, and knew he wasn't very convincing. And why should Eric want to meet him? Surely Eric would resent his presence under Honey's roof. But the friendly smile the other man offered looked sincere.

"I hear you had an accident today," Eric said, nodding toward Lucas's bandaged foot. "I hope it's nothing serious."

Lucas shook his head. "I'm sure it's just a minor sprain."

"Vera says he'll need to stay off of it for several days," Honey said, coming to stand next to Eric. "I insisted he remain here until it's better."

Lucas studied the younger man's eyes for a reaction and got none. He looked from one to the other and it hit him suddenly what a good-looking couple they made, both blond, both of them tan from working outdoors. He wondered how much time Eric spent with Todd and Melissa, and he wondered if he had ever been mistaken for their father, since they were as blond as he was. The thought upset Lucas so much, he couldn't keep from grinding his teeth. And while the two made small talk, Lucas had the insane urge to jump to his feet and demand to know if they were involved. The thought ate at his gut the way the ulcer already had, and he was thankful when Vera appeared at the door and announced dinner was ready. Thankful, that is, until Eric stepped forward and offered to assist him.

"I'm not a cripple," Lucas said, turning down his offer. He shoved himself up from the couch and hobbled to the door.

Eric nodded. "Of course not. I just don't want you to injure yourself further. We've no idea how serious it is. Honey says you refused to go to the doctor. Perhaps you'd allow me to take you tomorrow. We have insurance for this sort of thing, you know."

Lucas paused in the hallway. "Oh, I get it now. You're afraid I'm going to sue you."

"Lucas!" Honey stepped forward, between the two men. She glared at him. "Stop this right now. You will not come into my house and treat a guest of mine rudely."

"It's okay, Honey," Eric said. "I'm sure he didn't mean anything."

Lucas read the disappointment on Honey's face and knew he'd put it there. It was up to him to wipe it away. "Honey's right," he said at last. "I've no right to be rude. I apologize for what I said." He paused and shrugged, feeling like a schoolboy who'd been properly scolded. "I'm just feeling frustrated because of all I have to do and can't, now that I'm going to be laid up for a couple of days." He offered his hand. "Can we start over?"

Eric didn't hesitate. "Of course." He took Lucas's hand and shook it once more. "Now, what's all this pressing business you have to attend to?" he asked once they'd reached the dining room and he'd pulled a chair out for Lucas. "Maybe it's something I can help you with."

Lucas didn't know what to make of the other man's offer. Was Eric really trying to be friendly, or was he truly afraid of a lawsuit, as Lucas had first suspected? Perhaps he was trying to assist Lucas so he could get him out of the way and out of Honey's hair. "I have a lot of work left to do on my house," Lucas finally said. "You know, I want it ready for when Todd and Melissa return from camp."

"Excuse me one second," Honey interrupted, "and let me see if I can help Vera in the kitchen." She disappeared through a swinging door.

"What do you have to do?" Eric asked, once seated in his own chair.

"Oh, I need to finish painting and hang drapes on the windows, I guess," Lucas said. "And I have to buy furniture—not that I know much about picking out that sort of stuff."

"I know what you mean. I had to ask Honey to help me with my place. You should ask her to give you a hand."

"I did, but she refused." Lucas had barely gotten the words out of his mouth before Honey pushed through the swinging doors carrying a pot roast surrounded by vegetables. Eric didn't waste any time questioning her.

"How come you won't help Lucas decorate his place?" he asked.

The question took Honey off guard, and she stopped in her tracks. "What?"

"He needs someone to select furniture and draperies. Why don't you give him a hand?"

Honey swung her glance in Lucas's direction, and he could tell she wasn't happy that he'd reopened the subject, especially in front of her business partner. She laughed nervously. "I'm not an interior decorator, Eric."

"Yes, but you did a fine job with my place."

"I even offered to pay her," Lucas said, and was rewarded with a dark look from Honey.

"He's worried he won't have the place ready by the time Todd and Melissa get back," Eric told her, "and with his bad foot and all—"

"Okay, okay!" Honey said sharply. "I'll help." She shoved the pot roast in Lucas's face. "Won't you have some?" she offered between clenched teeth. Lucas had succeeded once again in getting his way, she thought, this time using Eric as an ally. She wondered if Eric had any idea he was being used. No, Eric was too nice a guy to understand the levels to which Lucas would stoop to get what he wanted out of life. She could tell Eric, of course, but he might think she was exaggerating, and he might accuse her of judging Lucas too harshly. She'd known Eric long enough to know that he insisted on giving folks a fair shake in life, since he had been treated unfairly at times. Eric might even accuse her of running from Lucas again, and she didn't want that, because it was too close to the truth.

Honey took a deep breath and waited for Lucas

to serve himself from the platter she'd handed him. He looked so innocent that no one would ever have believed what a conniver he was, and Honey itched to slap that look off his face. Oh, he knew what he was doing all right, she thought. He may fool Eric, but he would never fool her. Instead of saying anything, though, she smiled sweetly. She would not let him have the pleasure of knowing how trapped she felt.

"Of course I'll help you, Lucas," she said at last. "In fact, I was thinking of offering my help now that you've hurt yourself. I'll call a couple of painters in the morning, and we'll go to the furniture store as soon as your foot is better. How's that?"

Lucas nodded. "Thanks, Honey. I really appreciate it." It was all he could do to keep from grinning from ear to ear.

Dinner went well, and much to his surprise, Lucas found he liked Eric. That didn't mean he didn't watch every move the man made. Lucas spent much of the evening studying gestures and eye contact, looking for anything that might suggest a romantic relationship between the two. If the two had something going on, though, they were discreet. Only when Eric began to speak of his homeland did Lucas get truly concerned. It was obvious the man missed his country and his family. At one point, Honey reached over and covered Eric's big hand with her own, and Lucas almost choked on a mouthful of pot roast. After a moment, he excused himself and reclaimed his spot on the sofa in the next room.

Lucas decided that if Honey was involved with Eric, he certainly didn't want to have to witness it. She had every right, of course, since they were divorced, but that didn't make it easier to accept. Did they sleep together? he wondered. Did Eric know her as intimately as he had during their five years together? Lucas felt his gut tighten at the thought. He couldn't imagine Honey belonging to any man but him.

It was still early when Eric said good night, and Lucas was glad to see him leave. Honey joined him in the den once she'd helped Vera straighten the kitchen. "I wish I could convince Vera to retire," she confided after taking a chair directly across from him. "She's getting too old to take care of all of us, but every time I suggest it, she informs me she has enough spit and vinegar left to last another few years." Honey saw the photo albums on the coffee table. "I see you've been looking at pictures of Todd and Melissa," she said. She also saw that he was in a quiet mood.

"Yeah. They're really growing up."

"You should see how quickly they go through their school clothes," Honey said, and laughed.

Lucas wondered if having to buy clothes was a hardship for her, but he didn't dare ask. He sent a healthy check every month, but he was certain it wouldn't help much if she was having serious financial problems. "I've missed them," he said at last. He shrugged. "I guess I didn't realize how important they were to me until they were gone." His gaze met Honey's across the room. "Tell me about them."

Six

After a moment, Honey smiled and settled more comfortably in the chair. She liked talking about Todd and Melissa, enjoyed bragging and showing snapshots to people. She was certain she bored the pants off most folks. At least with Lucas she could feel comfortable boasting about them.

"Well, let me see," she said. "I've already told you that Todd plays Little League."

"What position?"

"Third base. He wanted to pitch, but the coach doesn't feel he's good enough."

Lucas listened and wondered if it bothered his son not to be able to pitch as he wanted. He couldn't imagine what an eight-year-old boy thought about, what his needs were. He had been so absorbed in his own needs, he had never considered his son's. Or his daughter's. Lucas flinched inwardly. Or his wife's, he added silently.

"He wants to be in Cub Scouts this year," Honey went on. "And Melissa wants to be a Brownie as soon as she's old enough. They both enjoy things like that. They enjoy the outdoors. Which is why I let them go on this camping trip with the church, despite my reservations."

"Reservations?"

"I'm afraid I balked at the idea of letting Melissa go at first. I didn't think she was old enough."

"Well, she is a bit young," he said thoughtfully.

Honey nodded in agreement. "I can't tell you how nervous I was . . . still am. But I decided I had to give her some freedom, even as young as she is. I don't want her to grow up like—" She stopped. "I don't want to be one of those overprotective parents."

Lucas knew Honey was referring to her own childhood, and the thought made him sad. "I'm sure she'll be okay, Honey," he said after a moment.

"I'm hoping she'll make friends," Honey went on. "She's rather shy and has trouble getting along with other children. I was sort of wishing she would open up a bit."

Lucas chuckled. "I can't imagine Melissa being shy," he said. "She always seemed so friendly and outgoing. I think she was a daddy's girl," he added proudly. "I can remember when she was a baby and wouldn't quiet down, I would just take her into the den with me, and we'd listen to music. She'd fall asleep in my arms every time."

Honey wanted to remind him of the times he hadn't been around to quiet his daughter, and of the times Melissa had peered out the window as a toddler, waiting for her daddy to come home at the end of the day. Instead of saying anything, though, Honey went on with the conversation at hand.

"Melissa doesn't seem to *want* to play with other children, and when she does, she often fights with them. I don't know if she does it for attention or what, but it keeps her in trouble at school." Honey saw the look of concern on his face and wondered if she'd made a mistake by telling too much. Of course, Lucas was bound to find out about Melissa's problems sooner or later, and he did have the right to know. But she was truly torn about how much she should tell him.

"It's nothing serious, is it?" he asked.

Honey shrugged. "I don't know," she said, being deliberately vague.

"You don't know?"

"I honestly have no idea, Lucas." At the troubled look he shot her, she decided she would have to level with him. "I've got her scheduled to see a behavior specialist in Fort Worth in three weeks."

"What the hell is that?"

Honey stiffened slightly. "A child psychologist."

Lucas straightened on the sofa. "You're sending a six-year-old to a child psychologist, for Pete's sake!" He didn't give her a chance to answer. "Good Lord, Honey. Isn't that a bit drastic?"

Honey leveled her gaze at him. "I don't think so. And believe me, I've thought long and hard about it. But Melissa is having other problems. She takes things that don't belong to her."

"Well, what kid doesn't?" he said, waving the remark aside as though it held about as much importance as the loose change in his pocket.

"It's gotten to be a habit with her, Lucas. Not only does she take things from the house, she takes things from school and from her teachers. I can't go into a store with her without watching her every minute to make sure she doesn't take something."

"She's probably looking for attention, Honey. Now that you're working and all, you probably don't get to spend as much time with her. Either of them," he added.

"I knew you'd blame it on my working," Honey said calmly, but she could feel her irritation returning, as it had over dinner when he'd involved Eric in his scheme to get her to decorate his house. "It never occurred to you that you might have contributed to the cause."

"How can I be the cause? I've only seen the kid a few times over the past year."

"Exactly."

Lucas could feel his anger rising, and he swung his feet onto the floor and planted his elbows on his knees. "Don't try to put this monkey on my back, Honey," he said tersely. "I've tried to see the kids as often as I could over the past year. If you had stayed in Houston, where it was more convenient for me—"

"Convenient!" She came to her feet in one fluid move, her cheeks flaming the same color as her blouse. "Convenient!" she repeated more forcefully. She planted her hands on her hips. "It wasn't *convenient* for you when they were living right under the same roof, Lucas."

He stood as well, forgetting his foot for a moment. "Well it's sure as hell not convenient with them living halfway across the state. And I can't just leave town on weekends like most folks, since I show a lot of property on those days."

"Yes, I remember clearly how many weekends you spent working," she said hotly. "Not to mention the other five days a week. And nights. Let's not forget how many nights you had to work, Lucas."

He balled his hands into fists at his side. "It was my job, Honey."

"No, Lucas, it was your life."

Lucas almost shouted the next words. "I made a mistake, okay!" Honey visibly flinched, and he sank to the couch. "It was my job, Honey," he repeated. "It wasn't as if I were cheating on you or sitting in a bar somewhere, drunk. I was working, trying to make a living for my family. At least give me credit for that."

Honey softened and sank onto her chair as well. "I do give you credit for that, Lucas," she said. "I know you did the best you could, and I appreciated it."

He looked at her. "Obviously not enough," he said sourly. "You walked out on me."

"I got tired of being alone," she said simply. "I got tired of spending all day and all evening with our babies, then when you finally *did* come home, of watching you fall asleep on the sofa, because you were too exhausted to do anything else. I got tired of not having a life. I resented the fact that I was the sole caretaker of our children. Before they were born, I dreamed of us doing things together with them, of going to the park and having picnics. I resented the fact that you got to dress up every day and go out into the real world and meet interesting people and do interesting things while I sat home with babies. Not that I didn't enjoy our children," she added quickly, "but I had no outlet. I was so confined and isolated and . . . lonely. I was living the same kind of life I had growing up. Do you know what that's like, Lucas? Do you know what it's like not having anyone you can really talk to? Do you know what it's like to have dreams, then have to put those dreams on a shelf because you're trying to do what's right or to please others? Do you know what it's like not being able to make a decision without someone else's approval? I was twenty-five years old at the time, and I didn't know the first thing about life." She had to stop to catch her breath.

"Oh, and I suppose now you do."

She inched her chin upward. "I know how to take care of myself," she said. "And my children."

He wanted to respond, but didn't. He wanted to tell her he knew she was broke, but no matter how much male pride shoved him in that direction, he refused to budge. It would only hurt her or perhaps push her farther away. Instead, he merely shook his head and gave a snort. "Life is really funny, you know that, Honey?"

"How do you mean?"

"Well, you work day and night until you think you're going to drop. And for what?" he asked suddenly. "What does it matter. In the end, you're going to end up the same. Alone and afraid."

"Afraid of what?" Her interest was piqued. It was the second time in so many hours that he'd mentioned being afraid, and now she had to know why.

Lucas's expression was packed with emotion. "I'm afraid I've lost you forever," he finally said. Honey looked away quickly, but he went on. "When I think back to how good it was between us, I get scared because I don't think I'll ever have it that good again. And some of it was very good, Honey, no matter what you say." He paused and followed her gaze to the window, where she was looking out. He wondered why she was having such a difficult time looking at him. "Sometimes I wish we'd never gotten together," he added after a moment.

Honey was surprised. "Why?"

He shrugged. "Then it wouldn't be so hard living as I do today. I wouldn't constantly be reminded of what I was missing out of life. I think it's better not knowing."

"If we hadn't gotten together, we wouldn't have Todd and Melissa," she said, feeling sad at the thought. She had never seen this side of Lucas. He appeared vulnerable and exposed. She wanted to go to him, hold him and comfort him, but she knew it would be dangerous.

"You're right," he said. "We have Todd and Melissa." He smiled softly, thinking about his children as he so often did these days. He would be glad to see them again. They gave unconditional love, simply because he was their father. He couldn't expect that from Honey. "Nobody can ever take them from me," he said. He pushed himself to a standing position, feeling more tired and weary than he had in months. Seeing Honey and Eric together had put a big strain on him. He had so many questions, but he knew he had no right to ask them. At this point, the only rights he had left were those directly relating to his children.

He would fight Honey about sending Melissa to a shrink, he told himself. He would not have his little girl tagged as different because she had trouble getting along with other children. Besides, Melissa was smarter than most kids her age—no wonder she grew bored and fought with them.

Honey would naturally see it as a form of aggression, when all it really meant was the child knew how to assert herself with others. Honey, of all people, should appreciate the fact that Melissa could stand up for herself. The separation of her parents had probably been a sobering experience for a three-year-old, he thought, and promised himself he would try to make up for it when Melissa returned. Another thought nagged him. He wondered if Honey was so strapped for money, she never bought toys. It would be only natural for a child to take what she couldn't have.

He wasn't going to bring all that up tonight, though, Lucas told himself. Not when he had other things on his mind, not when all he could think of was Honey and Eric together, laughing and talking intimately, Honey touching his hand. He wasn't sure he could face what existed between the two, just as he wasn't certain he could face life without Honey. For three years he'd let himself believe their separation was temporary. Even though he'd been stunned to receive divorce papers, he knew in his heart he could turn it around eventually, as he'd done in his work so many times before. It was the ultimate challenge. He hadn't counted on another man entering the picture, though, and that could very well destroy all his plans. He'd let his emotions block his clear thinking, something he never did in business. He'd convinced himself that Honey could not possibly love another man after what they'd been through together. Now he wasn't certain of anything.

"I think I'll go to bed now," Lucas finally said. He didn't want to argue with Honey anymore, and he certainly didn't want to dredge up the past. He needed time to think and plan his strategy. And he had to take his mind off Honey for a bit—Honey and Eric. It would drive him crazy if he let it. He could go off the deep end, do something foolish. It frightened him to think he might lose his head over any woman.

Remembering his foot suddenly, Lucas hobbled toward the door. "G'night, Honey," he said, almost sadly, and was gone.

Honey sat there wondering what to do next. Should she go to Lucas and try to talk, or just leave him alone? She had never seen him looking so forlorn, and it scared her. And she had never suspected he'd missed the children so badly. Once again, she wondered if she had been unfair to pick up and leave Houston and take their children halfway across the state, making it difficult for Lucas to visit. She had been so concerned with her desire to escape that she hadn't given much thought to what the separation would do to him. He'd been so busy, she hadn't thought it would matter much.

Honey stood and paced the floor. Lucas hadn't deserved it, she told herself. No matter what their relationship had been as husband and wife, he hadn't deserved having his children yanked from him without warning. And what about Todd and Melissa? Had she hurt them equally as much?

It irked her that Lucas would accuse her of overreacting by sending Melissa to a counselor, when he didn't fully understand the circumstances. How like Lucas to second-guess her when she'd agonized over the decision for weeks. Of course, he had that right as a parent, and maybe Melissa *would* settle down now that he'd be seeing her more. But she had wanted him to support her decision regardless, or at least discuss it with her instead of flying off the handle and telling her how wrong it was. And it irked her even more that Lucas had placed the blame on her career. What did he know of trying to balance a job and family? How many times had he missed a lunch appointment to meet with a teacher or participate in some school event?

But Lucas had his own way of thinking, she knew, and his opinions weren't always the correct ones. In the past, she would have acted on his suggestions whether she agreed or not. Now she knew her opinion was equally important.

Honey tried to sleep that night but couldn't, despite being so tired. Finally, she turned on the lamp and sat staring at the bedroom, which had once belonged to her mother. Vera had insisted she move into the room upon her return, a room that had fascinated her as a child but now appeared ugly, with its elaborate baroque-style furniture and heavy drapes of sky blue and gold. Honey preferred simpler styles, and she sometimes found herself wondering about the ancestors who had selected such ostentatious furnishings.

Major had almost had a fit once when she'd suggested redecorating the house so that it would look more like a home than a museum. Once she'd officially received her inheritance, which naturally had included the mansion, she'd discovered there wasn't the money to change it. She had, however, made changes to Todd and Melissa's rooms, hanging brightly colored posters on their walls, taking down the oppressive draperies that had blocked out years of sunlight and packing them into storage, where she hoped they would remain forever.

She thought of her mother, who'd spent the last year of her life in this room, staring at the scrolled ceiling, and she wondered if the woman had ever been happy. Vera had told her very little about her mother, only that she was the prettiest girl in five counties, with hair that looked as though it had been plucked from the sun and set upon her head. Honey did not remember Lacy Buchannan as being pretty, however. The woman Honey remembered had appeared frail and shrunken, her gold hair as dull and lifeless as the eyes that had peered back at her as a child. Honey had not known what strange ailment her mother had died of at the time, only that she had "wasted away." Lacy Buchannan's passing hadn't seemed to make much of a difference. One day she was there, and the next day she was not.

Honey stared at the ceiling for a while longer, wondering what it would be like to lie there in bed day after day and not care about life anymore. Had her mother had dreams and desires? Had Major squashed them under his boot just as he'd tried to do to hers? The thought made her sad. It also made her hate Major a little bit.

Honey shoved the bedclothes aside and swung her long legs from the bed. She refused to feel bad for the woman who'd once occupied that same bed. Besides, Lacy Buchannan had made her decision to die long before she'd drawn her last breath. She should have fought harder, Honey thought, instead of giving up.

Without bothering to locate her bathrobe, Honey

hurried out of the room and down the dimly lit stairway, not wanting to spend another minute thinking of the past. Some people lived in the past, and it fouled up their whole lives. She preferred to use it as a learning tool for the future. And she didn't really *hate* Major as much as she pitied him. She truly felt sorry for him, because he had been incapable of giving or receiving love. It wasn't her fault he hadn't loved her. She hadn't been unlovable, as she had thought growing up. Vera had taught her that. Vera had loved her enough for both parents.

Honey pushed the unpleasant thoughts from her mind, but she was trembling as she made her way across the dining room easily in the dark. After spending almost her entire life in the house, she knew her way by heart. She knew every nook and cranny, where the carpet was most worn, the drapes especially faded from a sun trying desperately to peek through. She kept the drapes up for privacy, but one day, when she had time and money, she planned to pull down those oppressive draperies and install new ones that would make the rooms light and airy. She wanted her children to have plenty of sunshine in their lives.

Honey pushed through the swinging doors and stepped into the kitchen. She came to an abrupt halt when she spotted Lucas standing before the open refrigerator.

"What are you doing here?" she asked, her tone slightly accusing.

Lucas, dressed in jeans and bare from the waist up, straightened and pulled a carton of milk from the refrigerator. "Raiding your refrigerator," he said. "Do you mind?"

"N-no. Help yourself." Suddenly, she wished she had slipped on her robe before coming down. Although her pale purple nightie wasn't overly revealing, it was short and snug enough to make her self-conscious in front of Lucas. The best thing to do, she decided, was act natural. She would just get what she came for and leave.

Lucas held up the milk carton, even as his gaze greedily devoured her. "Would you like some?"

"No thanks." Honey tried to gather her composure. Why did he insist on running around bare chested, for heaven's sake? She tried not to notice the way his jeans rode low on his lean hips, so low, in fact, his navel was clearly evident, as was the black hair that whorled around it enticingly and plunged beneath his belt buckle. He hadn't bothered to fasten his belt before coming down, she noticed. It taunted her. He'd never looked sexier, standing in the small circle of light from the refrigerator. That same dim light painted shadows on his face, emphasized the taut muscles on his back and shoulders, and darkened the hollows. Honey reached for the light switch near the door and turned it on, wanting to put an end to the intimacy. Lucas winced, then closed the refrigerator.

Honey reached into a cabinet and pulled out two clean glasses. "Here." She offered him one. His knuckles brushed hers as he took it, and she tensed.

"Couldn't sleep?" Lucas asked as he filled the glass, but his gaze remained fixed on her short nightgown. When had Honey begun wearing purple? he wondered. He decided he liked the color on her, the way it emphasized her golden complexion

and made her eyes appear almost lavender in the
light. And he *definitely* liked the fit, the way it
clung to her hips and breasts suggestively and
dipped at the waist, showing her figure to advan-
tage.

Honey shook her head. "No."

He set the carton on the cabinet and took a swig
of the milk. "All wound up, huh?" He sounded
amused. Honey shot him a cautious look, and his
own look sobered instantly. "Me too. Wonder why
we're so . . . tense?" he asked.

"I've no idea." Honey reached into a cabinet next
to the sink and pulled out a bottle of brandy. She
poured a liberal amount into her glass and put it
to her lips. When she spotted him staring at her,
she paused. "What are you looking at?"

He shrugged. "This is the first time I've ever seen
you take a drink. When did you start?"

"I didn't actually *start* anything," she said testily.
"I simply have one now and then when I can't
sleep." She took a sip, but she was uncomfortably
aware that he was staring. "Would you like one?"

"Naw, I gave it up. I prefer milk these days," he
added, toasting her with his milk glass.

"Good for you." She took another sip.

"That stuff will rot your gut out if you let it," he
went on, thinking what booze and hard living had
done to his own stomach—which was why he was
drinking milk. He'd left his medicine at home.
Besides, he wasn't about to let Honey know he had
physical problems. "Why don't I make you some
hot cocoa?" he suggested, going to a set of cabinets near the stove. "Surely you have some on
hand."

"I don't want hot cocoa."

He didn't seem to be listening as he began searching through the cabinets for the brown container. "Remember how I used to make you hot cocoa when you were pregnant and couldn't sleep?" He found what he was looking for and pulled it from the shelf. "And then after you drank it, I'd rub the small of your back until you became drowsy." He smiled as he searched for a pot in which to heat milk. "You'd curl up in my arms like a contented cat and—"

"Lucas, you're not listening to me!" she said loud enough to make them both jump. He swung his head around to look at her, his brown eyes surprised. "Can't you stop talking long enough to hear what *I* have to say?" she demanded. "Can't you, for once in your life, listen to me?"

He shrugged. "Sure, Honey. I just thought—"

"You just thought. You just thought," she said, waving her free arm wildly as she spoke. "You're always thinking. Not only for yourself, but for me. Well, I don't need you to think for me anymore, and if I prefer brandy over hot cocoa, I'll damn well drink it!"

"Fine, drink it."

She did. She turned the glass up and drained the liquid in one clean gulp. The liquid burned a path down her throat and landed in her stomach in a fiery ball. She was coughing and sputtering before the glass left her lips. Tears filled her eyes and streamed down her cheeks, and her face turned crimson.

"Feel better?" Lucas asked smugly.

"Much!"

"Great. Why don't you have another?"

"I think I might!" She reached for the bottle.

Lucas's hand closed around her own, effectively stopping her.

"What's the matter with you, Honey?" he demanded. "You're acting crazy, you know that?"

"Take your hand off me!"

"Not until you calm down. I'm not going to just stand here and let you do something foolish."

Their gazes locked, and for a moment the only sound in the room was their breathing, harsh and ragged. Honey's breasts rose and fell in cadence with the frantic beat of her heart. Lucas didn't miss it with his eyes. Neither did he miss the sight of her nipples, pert and erect, straining against the fabric of her gown. He felt his body go into a slow burn at the sight.

Finally, Honey loosened her grip on the bottle because she had no wish to turn the scene into a boxing match. Besides, she really didn't want another drink. Lucas placed it beside his milk glass and reached for a paper towel.

Honey, still holding the empty glass, felt a little silly. Her eyes continued to tear, but it wasn't from the brandy, she knew. It had to do with a lot of things: missing her children, her financial worries, and Lucas himself. She felt miserable, and she sniffed. She was only vaguely aware of Lucas standing before the sink, running water.

Lucas squeezed water from the paper towel and turned to her. "What's wrong Honey?" he asked gently. He raised the paper towel, and her eyes darted toward it cautiously. "I'm just going to clean your face," he said, hesitating. "You've got mascara everywhere." Then, while she remained as rigid as a statue, he dabbed her eyes with the moist cloth and chased a fat teardrop down her cheek, where it sank into the corner of her mouth. That same mouth had never looked more inviting to him, more tempting.

"Remember the last time I dried your tears?" he asked, smiling softly.

Honey forced her gaze from his, unable to meet his tender brown eyes. Of course she remembered. The thought made her stomach tense up. "No-no," she lied.

"When Melissa was born." He chuckled. "I don't mind telling you I was scared to death that night. Scared to death," he repeated.

Honey had to look at him. "Why?"

He shrugged and lowered his hand from her face, resting it comfortably on her shoulder. "Well, after what you went through with Todd. I felt like scum because I hadn't been able to attend all those birthing classes with you. I figured if I had, I could have done something for you that night. If I had been more involved and worked harder."

She was well aware of that game, the "what if" game she often played with herself. "I would've still had pain, Lucas," she said, a sudden wry amusement lurking through her tears.

"Yeah, but I could've made it easier for you if I had known what to do. Instead, I just yelled at the doctor for letting you suffer. It's a wonder he didn't throw me out." He sighed deeply. "Every time I've tried to help you, I've ended up hurting you instead," he said. His own eyes shimmered with emotion.

Without thinking, Honey touched his cheek. Her heart seemed to turn over in her chest at the sight of his pain. "Oh, Lucas, don't do this to yourself," she said. "It's in the past now. Let it go."

"It may be the past, but it sure as hell sealed my future," he said. He thought of Honey and Eric together again, seeing them as he had every time he'd tried to close his eyes that night. Even now it ate at his gut like an open wound, and he knew he could drink all the milk in the world and it wouldn't stop the pain.

Honey could feel her own eyes stinging with fresh tears. "It wasn't all your fault, Lucas," she said, trying to talk around a gigantic lump in her throat. "I should have put my foot down, *insisted* you spend more time with us. "I didn't know how. I didn't know how to go about getting what I wanted out of life."

Lucas raised his hands to her face, anchoring her jaw against his roughened palms. "I was your husband. I should have known what you needed."

"You couldn't have been expected to read my mind." The tears fell freely now.

Lucas felt as though his heart would break at the despair in her voice. Instinctively, he gathered her closer and pressed his lips against her forehead. When she didn't make a move to pull free, he tightened his hold on her, and the fabric of her gown caressed his sensitive inner arm. He kissed her damp eyelids and tasted her salty tears. In response, Honey sagged against him, her body warm and pliant. Lucas kissed the tracks her tears had made down her cheek and hesitated for one heart-shattering second before capturing her lips with his.

Seven

Honey stiffened only slightly as Lucas's mouth made contact with her own. Her lips parted, and his tongue slipped inside, seeking out the delights that for the past three years had existed only in his dreams.

The kiss was a direct contradiction to the one he'd planted on her several days before. That kiss had been hard and angry and demanding. This was a giving sort of kiss, nurturing, an offering of the best part of him. He lovingly reacquainted himself with the tastes and textures inside that were uniquely Honey, his tongue stroking slowly but thoroughly. He would not rush her, nor would he take more from her than she was willing to hand over. After a lifetime of taking, it felt right to give.

Even so, even though Lucas had convinced himself he had no intention of carrying the kiss any further, he would have had to be made of stone to ignore the very potent signals his body was giving him. He could not hold her in his arms without wanting her, without thinking what it would be like having her warm naked flesh against his, her soft breasts pressed to his chest. The thought sent a shock wave of desire through him, so strong, he shuddered. He snapped his head up with enough force to rattle his teeth. Honey was jarred back to reality by the abrupt movement.

She blinked. "What's wrong?"

Lucas stepped away and shoved his hands in his pockets to keep from reaching out for her once more. Control was quickly slipping from his grasp. He wanted her so badly, he hurt. She was still his woman, and he was half afraid that in another moment he might prove it if he didn't get himself in line. But he wouldn't force himself on her no matter how much he wanted her. He had learned the hard way that he could not take from her just because he desired it. He could not bend her will to his.

"It's late," he said. "I'd better walk you up to your room."

Honey was intensely disappointed. How good it had felt to stand there in his embrace, to feel his lips on hers, his powerful chest so solid against her breasts, his arms encircling her waist protectively. There were times she wanted to feel cherished and protected, she knew. There were days, when life was especially demanding, that she wanted a safe place to run to, a place where she could lock out the real world for a while, a warm place where she could forget her troubles.

She knew in her heart that place was in Lucas's arms.

Instead of saying anything, though, Honey simply turned and pushed through the swinging doors leading from the kitchen to the dining room. Lucas followed closely behind, groping in the dark to find his way. When he stumbled, Honey laughed softly and reached for him.

"Here, take my hand," she said. "I know this old house like I know my face. I'll show you the way."

Lucas took her hand, marveling at its softness. He was thankful she wore work gloves to protect her hands on the job. He closed his eyes briefly as images of those hands on his body assailed him. He followed her in the dark, thinking how odd it felt, how different for him to follow Honey after all the years he'd insisted on leading. A sense of vulnerability passed through him, but he realized it wasn't such a bad thing after all. His wife's grasp was strong and firm and sure, and he smiled. It was a heady, exhilarating feeling having Honey in control, even for something as simple as finding his way in the dark. He only hoped she could help him find a way back into her heart.

They reached the stairs, where a small night-light glowed from an outlet, and Honey released his hand. They took the steps slowly, as though both of them were anxious to prolong this time together, the easy camaraderie they now felt. But all too soon they reached the landing, and Honey made her way reluctantly to her bedroom door. When she raised her hand to the knob, Lucas's closed over it.

"Do you have to go inside?" he asked, his eyes almost pleading. "I mean, we could sit out here and talk for a bit." He motioned with his head to the padded bench against one wall. "Just for a little while," he added when she didn't answer.

"Talk about what?"

He shrugged, feeling like an inexperienced teenager on his first date. He had sold millions of dollars worth of property and convinced investors to take part in multimillion-dollar projects, but he had no clue as to how to talk his wife into spending a few minutes alone with him. He wore eight-hundred-dollar suits, traveled around Houston in a limo, and was treated like a king in all the best restaurants, but now it meant nothing. There he was, barefoot and wearing his oldest jeans, trying to court the love of his life. He didn't stand a chance. "Just talk," he said. "It seems I didn't get to know you when I had the opportunity."

Honey drew a long, shaky breath. "We can talk inside."

"Inside?" His face went blank. "You mean in your bedroom?" When she nodded, he chuckled and leaned close, propping his arm against the wall near her head. "Uh, I don't think that's a good idea, Honey. I'm afraid I wouldn't feel much like . . . talking." He laughed again, and the sound came from deep within his chest, low and husky, sending tingles along Honey's bare arms and shoulders. "When you invite a man into your bedroom, you'd better think about what you're getting yourself into," he cautioned, a wicked smile playing across his full lips. "It may not be safe." He was teasing her, he knew, but he was certain she had no idea what she was asking of him. To expect him to just sit cross-legged on her bed and talk to her as their children would was expecting a little too much. His control was too near the breaking point.

Honey leveled her gaze at him. "I'm a big girl, Lucas. Maybe I don't want to be . . . safe." She had the supreme pleasure of seeing that cocky, self-assured smile fade from his face before she turned and pushed through the door. And when she heard him stumble behind her, she smiled to herself, knowing the man had tripped over his own two feet. There was satisfaction in knowing that Lucas McKay wasn't as tough as he pretended to be.

Lucas was only vaguely aware that he had followed Honey into the room. He heard the door close and figured he must have closed it, but the solid click made him jump slightly. He muttered a curse under his breath for this sudden attack of nerves.

Lucas's gaze was trained on Honey as she walked gracefully across the room to her bed, her nightie swaying against the backs of her thighs as she moved. She paused directly in front of the lamp on her nightstand and faced him once more. With the light behind her, every delicate curve of her body was visible through the thin garment, and Lucas wondered if she was purposely goading him. The thought that she might be sent a tremor of delight through him. "Don't move," he whispered thickly. "Just stand there for a minute."

Honey complied, watching the look on his face as his gaze slowly climbed the length of her, starting at her trim ankles and graceful calves. He remembered her thighs as being the silkiest things he'd ever touched. He swallowed hard as he thought of what nestled between those thighs. He remembered that part of her as well, warm and musk scented, dusted with curls the color of burnished gold. His gut tightened, and every nerve in his body came alive. He clenched his hands at his side and gritted his teeth, certain this experience would win him a trip to the dentist. And then, in one graceful swoop, Honey lifted the nightie high over her head.

Lucas caught a glimpse of gently flexing muscles as she moved, and when the gown was tossed aside, he feasted upon the generous but well-proportioned curves that he'd known and loved so well—only they were nicer somehow, because she was in wonderful physical condition. He couldn't help but appreciate the firm lines and toned muscles. There wasn't an ounce of fat anywhere. For a moment, he could only gaze at her.

Lucas grinned suddenly, feeling like the veritable boy in the candy store. If she truly had invited him in to talk, she had made one serious mistake. "I don't know what game we're playing, Honey, but I sure as hell like the rules."

"It's not a game, Lucas," she said simply. "You and I both knew it was only a matter of time before we got together. Isn't that what you told me the first day you saw me?" She didn't wait for him to answer. "I suppose that's why I stayed with you for five years, why I put up with all that isolation and loneliness. I knew once we climbed into bed together you would notice me and love me."

"I've always loved you, Honey."

"But this is the only place you could really prove it to me, wasn't it?" she said, indicating the bed with a slight nod. "This is the only place where you could open up to me, where I could feel cherished." She stepped closer. "I'm not sure if this thing between us is healthy," she said on a small laugh, "but it has existed from the very beginning. It never died, Lucas. I want you as much today as I did before."

It was like music to his ears. Lucas could hardly believe what he was hearing. He closed the distance separating them, but he did not touch her, half afraid she might disappear in a puff of smoke. He gazed at her in adoration, drinking in the sight like a man who had thirsted for many years. And he *had* thirsted for the sight of her. He'd spent three painful years thirsting. Looking back now, he had no idea how he'd gotten through it.

"You were beautiful before, Honey," he heard himself say, "but now you're . . . devastatingly so." Finally, because he could not resist touching her any more than he could resist taking his next breath, he gathered her into his arms. As her breasts made contact with his chest, her nipples, already delightfully pointed, nestled in his chest hair. He closed his eyes and sighed, knowing he'd just gotten his first taste of heaven.

And when he kissed her, it was as if he were kissing her for the first time. Her mouth was a well of sweetness, and he sipped from her lips tenderly before dipping his tongue inside. He drank deeply of her, but it did not quench his need. The more he took from her, the more he needed for his very survival. It had always been that way for him where she was concerned.

The gentle stirrings he'd felt earlier concentrated in his loins, making him achingly aware of that part of himself that strained against his zipper. He nudged Honey instinctively, reached around and grasped her hips, and cradled her against him, so there was no doubt in her mind of his arousal.

He kissed her with a fervor and vengeance that told him he was in his element now, making love to his woman. Yes, *his* woman. She was his—every breath, every fiber of her being, her very essence belonged to him. She could divorce him as many times as she liked, but she would always belong to him.

Lucas slipped his hands from her hips and found her breasts. He moaned against her mouth as his thumbs located the stony hard nipples. His mouth left hers and closed over one eager nipple. Honey slipped her arms around his neck and held on, half afraid her knees would buckle. This is the part she remembered best, she thought, closing her eyes, letting her head fall back in complete abandon as he introduced her body to one wonderful sensation after another. She arched against him, feeling her lower belly warm under his touch. Somewhere deep inside she could feel the heat igniting a delicious sense of anticipation. By the time he'd kissed her other breast, she was overcome with yearning.

Lucas chuckled under his breath and in one fluid move swept her high in his arms. Nothing was going to stop him from making love to his wife now. The world could have stopped spinning for all he cared, and if someone had knocked on the door that very moment with a solution to world peace, he would have sent them away. He smiled down at her. Her eyes were smoky, her face flushed. He knew the signs well. He had not forgotten how she looked in passion, the sounds she made, the way her body trembled at his touch. It had sustained him through the years. Nor had he forgotten how to tease and torment her. He knew exactly the words that coaxed her on, and while she might insist afterward that they were a bit raunchy for her tastes, those same words often sent her flying over the edge, out of control. And he liked it when she lost control and whimpered his name against his lips. The thought made him burn for her now.

Honey read the look of determination in Lucas's eyes as he carried her to the bed and laid her on it. She saw the stark need and desire in those brown depths that glittered almost black in the lamplight. She had taunted him, she knew, by standing in front of the lamp in her gown, but she had purposefully done so once she'd decided to invite him to her bed. The first time they'd made love, she'd been a shy, quaking virgin who'd known nothing of how to please a man. This time it would be different, she told herself. This time she would meet him on common ground, give back as much pleasure as she received. Then Lucas released her, raised up, and reached for the fastening on his jeans. A moment later, he stood before her naked and magnificent. Honey's heart slammed to her throat, and she completely forgot the promises she'd just made to herself.

She opened her arms to receive him, and Lucas came without hesitation. The mattress dipped with his weight, and he was beside her. Arms and legs entwined, lips engaged, and a steady heat rose between them as their bodies were reacquainted.

Lucas nipped her earlobe with his teeth, then tongued the outer shell until Honey shivered. He chuckled softly, filled with the sheer joy of making love to his wife. He gazed down at her face. Her gold hair fanned across the pillow beneath her head, and he toyed with a fat curl. "I want to brush your hair," he said.

Honey couldn't have been more surprised. "N-now?"

He smiled. "Now. Where's the hairbrush?"

"On my dressing table." She couldn't conceal her disappointment entirely. How could he think of brushing her hair, when all she wanted to do was have him take her in his arms again and put an end to this sweet anticipation?

"Would you please get it for me?"

Honey blinked, once, twice, and again. He was serious. She automatically sought out her nightie and reached for it.

"Without the gown, if you don't mind," he said simply. When she started to protest, he tweaked her nose playfully. "I haven't seen my wife in three years. I want to now."

The look in his eyes was so engrossing that Honey didn't bother to remind him they were divorced. "Okay," she said finally, but her eyes gauged the distance between the bed and dressing table. She sighed inwardly. Lucas knew what he was asking of her, that even during a five-year marriage she had possessed a certain amount of modesty. While she might traipse about their bedroom in a bath towel or tease him unmercifully from behind a shower curtain, she had never been one to strut around completely naked. And she had to admit she was a bit self-conscious about her hips and thighs. While she knew she was in fairly good shape, she had never been thin and svelte like some women.

It wouldn't be easy, but she would do it.

Honey mustered up all the self-confidence she

had and pushed herself from the bed. Then, without wasting another second, she walked briskly but calmly to the dressing table on the other side of the room. Every insecurity came to life as she felt Lucas taking in her bareness. There was no towel, no robe, nothing but skin. She grabbed the brush like a lifeline and turned. She was not surprised to find him watching her.

"You have a dimple on the left side of your fanny," he said.

Honey felt her cheeks burn. She hitched her head high. "I know that," she said sharply. Inside, though, she was filled with uncertainty. Would he be turned off by a little bit of cellulite? she wondered, then grew indignant. She thought she looked pretty damn good, considering she was thirty years old and had given birth to two children.

Lucas, propped on his elbow, smiled. "And later, I'm going to kiss it," he promised.

The heat radiated to her chest as Lucas's words hit her with enough force to make her dizzy. Honey felt her stomach flutter wildly at the thought of Lucas's lips touching that part of her body. She felt vulnerable and exposed but very turned on by the man on the bed who could make love to her mind so expertly that by the time he actually touched her she was burning up. "And if you're a good boy, I might let you," she finally said, deciding two could play the game as well as one.

Lucas winked, and she wondered if he knew how devilishly sexy he looked lying there unabashed in his nakedness. "Oh, I'll be good, Honey. I'll be real good."

And she didn't doubt it for an instant.

Honey handed him the hairbrush. She sat on the edge of the bed, and Lucas moved closer. The brush slipped through her hair with ease as Lucas started at the very top of her head and ran it down her back. As she sat there, rigid, she could hear him breathing, feel his warm breath against her shoulders. She relaxed after a moment and closed her eyes, remembering a time when Vera used to brush her hair before bedtime. The act was soothing and comforting.

"When did you decide to grow your hair long?" he asked, his voice low and sensual at her ear.

She almost shivered at the sound. "I'm not sure. I just got tired of fussing with it. With it long I can wash it and let it dry on it's own. Before I had to work with it a lot."

"I like it."

"Thank you."

"Don't ever cut it."

She stiffened slightly, not sure she liked the way he had simply *told* her how to wear her hair—just the way he'd chosen her clothes and perfume and everything else in the past. She liked her hair long also, but she would shave her scalp rather than have him tell her how to wear it. "We'll see," she said.

"I'd like to pick wildflowers for you to wear in your hair," he went on, smiling to himself when he realized she hadn't appreciated his previous remark. "And one day when you have time, know what I'd like?"

"W-what?"

"I'd like for you to braid it with ribbons." He continued to brush as he spoke, his voice so low, Honey had to strain to hear it. "I remember seeing a young girl once who wore her hair that way, and I liked it. Would you do that for me sometime, Honey?"

He really could be a convincing stinker when he wanted to, Honey thought, feeling her stomach turn to mush. "Yes, well, maybe," she finally said.

Lucas parted her hair at her nape and pulled it aside, letting it fall over her shoulders to her breast. Then, very gently, he pressed his lips there. The downy hairs on the back of her neck prickled, and he chuckled. "I like the way your body responds to me, Honey." His lips reappeared on her shoulder, skimming one side lightly then the other. Honey closed her eyes and leaned her head to one side.

Lucas kissed her backbone, tonguing each tiny vertebra in his path until Honey broke out in goose bumps. She sat there, eyes closed, giving in to the wonderful sensations his touch evoked. One hand slipped around her waist and fell lightly onto her thigh, and as he continued to kiss her neck and ears, that very same hand tormented the silken area of her inner thigh. His hands were slightly rough as he caressed her, moving back and forth but never coming close to that part of her that was now literally burning for his touch. Finally, she whimpered in frustration, knowing she couldn't stand it much longer.

And then, thankfully, he moved his hand. He cupped her with his palm, and she sighed openly. A moment later, she felt his fingers slip inside, and the pleasure was so intense, she thought she would cry.

"You're wet, Honey," he said, a satisfied smile on his face.

"Yes." Eyes closed, she nodded.

His fingers dipped farther, and she gasped aloud as they explored. He pulled them out slightly and located the very crux of her desire. While his lips never stilled on her neck and earlobes, neither did his fingers on the elusive bud that brought her such pleasure. Honey could barely sit still as he worked his magic, as the heat converged into something wild and frenetic and finally burst into something white-hot and delicious. She threw her head back and cried out softly, and Lucas crooned in her ear, taking her to a place in her thoughts where she was certain no decent woman should go.

When her body quieted, Lucas laid her back on the bed gently. "I'm going to taste you now," he said as he kissed a path between her breasts, past her navel, and finally kissed that area that was ultrasensitive. And when she was, once again, caught up in the frenzy of sensations, Lucas entered her, driving himself deeply, enveloping himself in all that was her.

And he knew he had finally found his way home.

Honey awoke sometime later, held tight in Lucas's embrace. She knew he was in a deep sleep by the gentle, even breathing in her ear. She tried to move but couldn't; his arms circled her waist like a vise, his legs entwined with her own. He had always held on to her too tight, she thought, as though half afraid she might bolt. His body was big and warm and comforting, although it felt funny to share her bed with someone after three years of sleeping alone.

Honey finally disentangled herself from him and slipped out of bed, realizing with a slight blush that she was naked. She tiptoed across the room to one of the tall windows, the sound of her footsteps muffled by the room-sized rug. She pulled the heavy drape aside and peered out at the night sky, where the moon sat low on the horizon.

What had she done? Honey glanced over her shoulder at the sleeping man whose silhouette she could barely make out in the dark room. Inside, her heart thudded, and she felt a sense of dread washing through her body. Why on earth had she invited him into her room, when common sense and logic had warned her against it? Why had she opened her heart and emotions once more and let him in, when she knew it was dangerous? She hadn't been thinking rationally, she told herself. But then, she'd never had a rational thought in her life when it came to Lucas McKay. Logic and common sense vanished into thin air when he touched her.

What would he expect from her now? she wondered, now that she'd lain with him and shared those things that were too intimate to even discuss with good friends. Would he be willing to go on as though it had never happened? She doubted it. He would naturally want her back in his life. But what about the life she had worked so desperately to build without him?

She had made a serious mistake. By inviting Lucas to her bed, she had given him a very special part of herself, a part she'd never shared with another man. But Lucas would never be happy with that, she knew. He would want it all. He would demand not only her love and devotion but her dreams and thoughts and everything else that made up her existence. Just as he held her too tightly in the night, he would take hold of all that was hers. Like a skilled surgeon, he would cut away those parts of her that sought independence or chased after dreams that did not include him. He would mold her, once again, into the kind of woman he wanted for himself, and in the end she would not resemble the woman she was now.

Honey dropped the curtain into place and tiptoed back to the bed, very carefully climbing in so as not to wake him. She stayed to her side, literally hanging onto the edge to avoid touching him. After a moment, he moved closer, as though sensing her presence even in his sleep, and his big strong arms reached out and pulled her easily against him.

Honey felt her eyes sting with unshed tears. It felt so wonderful to lie against him. It would be sheer heaven to climb into bed with him each night, make love until they were both sated, and fall asleep in each other's arms. She loved him, she knew, a love that was as deep and consuming as it had been the day she'd married him. But that love had a price, and she was not willing to give up her very soul.

Honey felt Lucas stir beside her, and a moment later his hands skimmed her body. He arched against her, and her pulse quickened when she felt his hardness at her hip. He chuckled in the darkness and very gently turned her over so that she was facing him. In the night, he sought and found her lips and captured them with a hungry kiss, and she responded eagerly, straining against him, opening her mouth wide to receive his greedy tongue.

And when he thrust into her, Honey responded with an urgency she'd never known, because common sense and logic were too difficult to find in the dark.

Eight

When Lucas opened his eyes the following morning, he discovered it was after ten o'clock and he was alone. He called Honey, thinking she might be in the bathroom, but there was no answer. His heart sank as he touched the pillow beside him, where the imprint of Honey's head was still visible. Without wasting another second, he swung his legs off the bed and reached for his jeans and underwear.

Oh, what a night! Lucas grinned as he stepped into his jeans and fastened them. He stretched like a contented animal. And he was content, more than he'd been in months. He felt in harmony with the rest of the world and knew that if he could carry a tune in a bucket, he would probably burst into song. Love really made a fool out of some folks, he thought. His stomach growled, and he realized suddenly how hungry he was. He hadn't eaten much dinner the night before, and then, of course, he and Honey had worked hard through the night.

He grinned again. At the moment, he had only two things on his mind, finding Honey and getting something in his stomach.

Lucas felt his body stir at thoughts of Honey. He was just as hungry for her as he was for food. While food nourished his body, Honey offered nourishment to his very soul. It didn't matter that they had made love long into the night and that he'd awakened her shortly before dawn wanting her again. She had been soft and warm and yielding. He'd watched her sleep afterward, thinking again how much he loved her.

And Honey McKay was still in love with him, he told himself as he went into the bathroom and splashed cold water on his face. She hadn't said as much, but he knew deep in his heart she had never *stopped* loving him. He'd read it in her eyes when he'd thrust into her and she'd wrapped those silky legs around his waist.

Lucas's stomach growled again as he dried his face on a hand towel that carried her scent. It occurred to him then that Honey was probably downstairs preparing breakfast because she would be as hungry as he was. He left the room and took the stairs, two at a time, anxious to see his wife. Now that things were right between them, he would insist they be remarried right away. Of course, he'd never thought of himself any other way. In his mind, he was just as married to her as he'd been the day the judge had pronounced them man and wife at the Sweetbriar Courthouse.

Perhaps they'd take another honeymoon, he thought. They could go back to the same little hotel in Mexico. This time, though, he wouldn't grumble or make excuses when she asked to go sightseeing. Things would be different this time around, he promised himself. Honey had taught him well that he needed to respect her needs as well as his own. He liked this new Honey who thought enough of herself to make a few demands.

Lucas whistled as he made his way through the dining room and pushed through the swinging doors leading to the kitchen. The sound died in his throat when he spotted Vera standing over the kitchen sink.

"Where's Honey?" he asked, glancing around the room expectantly.

Vera looked up. "What do you mean, where's Honey? She's where she always is at this time of morning. Working."

"She went to work today?" he asked in obvious surprise.

"Is there any reason she shouldn't have?"

Lucas felt his excitement abate at the news, and it was difficult to keep his disappointment from showing. "Naw, I guess not. Did she say whether she would be working at my place today?"

Vera went back to her work. "She didn't say, and I didn't ask."

"Give me a break, Vera," he said on a sigh. "I know you have to have some idea where she went. Why do you make me work so hard for everything?"

The woman rolled her eyes and looked at him. "Look, I told you, I don't know nothing. All I know is Eric called and—"

"Eric called?" Lucas's backbone went rigid at the man's name.

"And she had to leave early to meet him. Now, do you want coffee or breakfast? You can't have cereal because some fool left the carton of milk out last

night and it spoiled." The look she gave him told
him she knew who the guilty party was.

"No, nothing," he said, his appetite suddenly
gone. He raked his hands through his hair. "Is
there a car around here I can borrow?"

"Nope."

"No car? Look, Vera, I know you have a car. I've
seen that old beat-up station wagon out front, and
I know it belongs to you."

"Yes, but I don't have a car you can borrow," she
repeated.

Lucas was quickly getting frustrated with the
situation. He had to find Honey fast. He had to
find out, once and for all, what Eric was to her.
Was there some specific reason Eric had called her
that morning? Lucas could not imagine Honey
spending a night of passion in his arms if she was
in love with another man, but he had come to
realize there were a lot of things he didn't know or
completely understand about his wife.

"Is there a taxi service in town?" he asked.

"Homer Beechum used to run a service, but he
got closed down for income tax evasion."

"So there's *nobody*?" he asked in disbelief.

"This ain't Houston, you know," she said. "We
don't have much use for buses and cabs and the
sort."

Lucas's impatience was quickly gaining momen-
tum. "Okay, how about I buy your car from you,
Vera?"

"It ain't for sale."

"I'll give you . . . say, eight hundred bucks for
it. That's twice what it's worth. What do you say?"

Her look was unyielding. "If I was considerin'

sellin' it, which I ain't, I wouldn't take less than fifteen hundred for it."

"Fifteen hundred dollars!" He almost shouted the words. She shrugged and turned back to the sink. "Okay, one thousand dollars," he said. "My final offer." When she didn't budge, he added, "The damn thing is probably going to break down on me before I get to where I'm going."

Vera pondered it, then dried her hands on a kitchen towel. "I'll get the keys."

Lucas showered in record time, then made the drive out to his house, cursing Vera's old car for all it was worth as it sputtered and bumped along the country roads. He was peeved at the price the old woman had insisted on, but there was nothing he could do. He had needed transportation, plain and simple.

When Lucas arrived at his place, he found Honey and Eric standing beside her old pickup truck, talking and looking through some papers she held in her hand. He felt his jaw tighten at the sight of them together as he parked Vera's car and climbed out.

Honey looked surprised to see him. "Lucas, how on earth did you convince Vera to loan you her car?" she asked.

"It's a long story," he said, closing the distance between the two. He nodded curtly at Eric. "Honey, I need to talk to you. Is there some place—"

"Your foot!" she said. "You're not limping any-more. And where's the bandage?"

Lucas winced inwardly. He'd completely forgotten about his foot. "Oh, it's much better now," he said. "I can walk on it just fine."

"You're not even limping this morning," Eric pointed out.

Honey leveled a frosty gaze at Lucas, knowing by the sheepish look on his face that she'd been duped. Her face reddened at the thought. "I'd say that was a fairly remarkable recovery, wouldn't you?"

Lucas could see that she wasn't pleased with him, and that made him more determined to get her alone and talk. "Honey, can we go into the house? I really do need to talk to you," he repeated.

"I need to talk to you too," she said. "Eric is going to start sodding your lot today."

"So soon?"

"Well, you said you were in a hurry. Anyway, a water main busted during the night at the subdivision where they've been working, so they can't do anything until it's fixed and the place dries out a bit." She had to stop to catch her breath. She was talking too fast because she was angry, angry that Lucas was obviously up to his old tricks. His foot wasn't any more injured than hers was. And to think what he'd put her through over it. Was there nothing the man wouldn't do to get his way? she wondered.

"So now we're in a quandary because we don't have any of your shrubbery in," she went on. "It's no big deal, of course. I just prefer having everything else done before the sodding begins. We're putting out fertilizer now, and I've marked off a spot out back for your garden and play area. But I really need you to decide on your shrubs and trees today."

Lucas was growing impatient with all the interruptions. "Do we really have to have a discussion *now*?" He wondered how she could possibly think of yard work at a time like this, when there were so many things he wanted to tell her.

Honey's look was point-blank. "Yes, we have to do it now," she said. "When you told me you were in a hurry, I took you seriously and hired extra help so it could be done quickly. Have you changed your mind?" She was growing irritated with him, and it showed. Here she was, making every effort to do his lot, and he was squirming as if he had ants in his pants. It would be difficult working with him now after spending the night with him. She had thought of little else all morning. But he didn't have to make things harder for her.

"I haven't changed my mind," he said, resolved that he would have to put things on hold for a moment. "What do I need to do?"

"You need to ride over to the store and choose what you want for your yard," she said simply. "We'll have to wait until fall to plant some of the trees, but you can decide on shrubs and flowers. Of course, I'll show you what will work best."

Lucas pondered it. He could talk to her on the way back to the store, he thought. Perhaps this was just a bad time for her, what with the men waiting to get started. It had to explain why she was acting so distant. "Yeah, okay, Honey," he agreed, knowing that when he got her in the truck alone, he would tell her once and for all what was on his mind. Perhaps they could drive over to the courthouse that afternoon and apply for a marriage license. After what they'd shared the night before, he was certain she would be as anxious as he was to get it settled between them.

"You can follow Eric and me in your car," she said.

He arched both brows. "What do you mean, follow you and Eric?" He shot a glance at the man in question. "I thought he was going to lay sod."

Eric stepped forward. "I've got enough men working on it," he said. "I'm going back with Honey to help. She can't very well lift the plants on her own."

"I can lift them."

"You?" Honey and Eric spoke simultaneously.

"Why not me?"

Eric shrugged. "Some of them are quite heavy."

Lucas shot him a cool look. "Do I look like a weakling to you?" Lucas realized he probably did look weak to a man that size.

Eric was quick to respond. "Of course not."

Honey cut in. "Lucas, this really isn't necessary. You're a paying customer. We certainly don't expect you to do the work as well."

"Yeah, but I've sort of put you on the spot because I'm in such an all-fired hurry. The least I can do is help out. I'll feel guilty if you don't let me, Honey." He knew in his heart that guilt had nothing to do with it. He didn't want Honey and Eric to spend too much time alone.

Honey relented. "Oh, okay, Lucas," she said begrudgingly as she made her way toward the truck. "I don't know why I try to argue with you. You've always had your own mind."

"Ready to go?" Eric asked, turning for the truck as well.

"I'm ready," Lucas replied, gazing at him squarely, knowing he would do anything to get the man out of Honey's life.

• • •

The morning passed quickly for Lucas, who followed Honey around like a lost puppy as she helped him choose greenery for his yard. "You really don't have to decide on everything today," she said.

"I didn't realize there were this many kinds of shrubs," he told her, wondering how she knew so much about each individual species. She talked about them as if they were her children, pointing out each characteristic and where they would look and grow best in his yard.

"Oh, there are hundreds of varieties," she told him, "but I only keep the most popular on hand." She led him to a new bunch. "I'd recommend you set these in that spot where you're having erosion problems," she said. She fingered one of the healthy leaves. "These boys like full sun and should do wonderfully for you."

"What are these?" Lucas asked, pointing out a grouping of shrubs with flowers.

"Azaleas. I was thinking of using several colors for that garden of yours. And maybe a few gardenias. Here's one over here. Come smell the flowers."

Lucas followed her, drinking in the sight of her firm behind as she walked. She wore navy shorts and a sleeveless white blouse that looked crisp and bright against her tanned arms. Honey stopped before a bush and picked a small white flower.

Lucas took the blossom from her and raised it to his nose and sniffed. "Hm, nice," he said, his gaze meeting hers. "But I prefer the way you smell."

Honey glanced away. "Yes, well, I think you've

chosen wisely for your yard. Later, we'll add some flowering trees and—"

Lucas glanced around to make sure Eric was busy inside. "Honey, what's going on?" he demanded. "Why are you treating me as if I've got something that's catching?"

"I don't know what you mean."

"You've hardly looked at me, and every time I get close, you move away. Are you beginning to regret what happened between us last night?"

"Last night has nothing to do with this, Lucas. But yes, I have doubts about whether I did the right thing by inviting you into my bedroom."

"Didn't you enjoy it?"

She blushed. "Of course I did."

"Then what's the problem?"

There were too many problems to name, she wanted to tell him, but didn't because she was in a hurry. "I'm not sure it was a good idea. We're divorced now, and we have our own lives."

"That's one problem that can be solved right away."

"What do you mean?"

He stepped closer and tucked the flower carefully behind her ear. She stiffened slightly at the close contact, but didn't say anything. "Maybe you and I should take a drive to the courthouse, Honey," he said. He dropped his hands to her shoulders. "We can get a license and be married in a couple of days."

She took a step back, effectively breaking the hold he had on her. She gave a little nervous laugh, but refused to meet his gaze. "Lucas, what are you talking about?"

Lucas frowned. "It should be obvious. I'm talking about you and me getting together again, baby. I'm asking you to be my wife . . . again."

Honey stiffened. She should have seen it coming, but she hadn't. She'd been so caught up in the realities of what had passed between them the night before that she hadn't been able to think straight since awakening that morning. Knowing she still loved him scared her silly, scared her because she realized how much control Lucas had over her. In bed he'd proven once and for all he was master. He would always want the upper hand with her, though—not just in bed, but in every aspect of her life. Slowly but surely, he would take complete control.

"I've already told you, Lucas," she finally said, "I'm not interested in marriage."

"Yes, but that was before last night."

"I don't care about last night—"

"What do you mean, you don't care about last night?" he asked, his face a mask of disbelief.

"I'm simply not going to tie myself down again. I'm perfectly happy the way I am."

"Oh really, Honey?" he said, clenching his fists at his side. It never occurred to him that she would turn his offer down flat. "Are you content to live in that big dark house and sleep in an empty bed the rest of your life?"

"Are you presuming I need a man in my life to make me happy?"

"Not just any man. Me."

"I have a good life, Lucas. I have a job I like and two beautiful children—"

"Two children who need a father."

"They had one once, remember?" She went on, knowing that she didn't have to remind him of all his shortcomings as a husband and father. "I'm not going to marry simply for Todd and Melissa's benefit. They are doing quite well with things as they are. They are happy, thriving children. Sure, Melissa has her problems, but nothing that can't be worked out. I'm not going to risk their happiness because you and I have a grand time between the sheets. I'm not going to ever put myself in the position I was in before."

"I told you I've changed. Things will be different this time."

"Yes, but I still see the same ol' Lucas who will do anything to get what he wants in life. Including having his yard bulldozed, faking an injury, and heaven only knows what else."

"I did it out of love, Honey. Because I wanted you back so damn much."

"That's right, you did. But you never once stopped to consider what *I* wanted, did you? Or what *I* needed."

"After last night I thought I had a fairly good idea," he said sharply, then had the pleasure of seeing her blush again. "I guess I was wrong. I guess maybe you've changed too."

"You just can't handle it when things don't go your way, Lucas. You never could."

"That's not true," he all but shouted. "If that were true, I would never have let you walk out on me three years ago and take my children with you."

"Did you expect divorce to be fun?"

"No, but I expected to have some rights. My life was irrevocably changed right before my eyes, and there wasn't a damn thing I could do about it. It was unfair, Honey, more unfair than anything I could ever have done to you." He was prevented from talking when Eric suddenly appeared, looking somewhat embarrassed that he'd caught them arguing.

"Are we ready to load the truck?" he asked Honey.

Honey refused to meet her partner's gaze. She knew he would be concerned if he saw she was upset. "Yes, I think we have everything," she said. She shot Lucas one last glance before she joined Eric.

Lucas worked that day with a vengeance he didn't know he possessed, because it helped him not to think. He didn't want to think about how loving Honey had been the night before, and just when everything seemed okay between them, how she'd refused his marriage offer that very morning. Who was he kidding? he asked himself. Hard work didn't stop him from thinking about it, it only helped him deal with it. His frustrations were channeled into physical activity, backbreaking labor, when what he really wanted to do with all that adrenaline was shake Honey till her teeth rattled, until he could make her see things his way. He knew those days were over, though. Honey had a mind of her own now.

Working alongside Eric, he dug hole after hole, and continued to dig even when Eric made another trip back to the store for more greenery. He ignored Honey completely, deciding it was best not to say anything for the time being. Inside, he was an emotional wreck.

For one thing, he felt a little foolish for thinking that after one night of passion Honey would be only too happy to run up to the courthouse and become his wife once again. How could he have been so dumb? he wondered as he sank another shrub into the ground as Eric had shown him. Thinking of the man set his teeth on edge, and he wondered again if Eric Severnson had anything to do with Honey's reluctance to remarry him.

By the end of the day, Lucas could not believe the changes in his yard. Although there was a lot of work left, his entire lot had been sodded and most of the shrubs were in place. Honey had located a wonderful old wooden fence out back and had Eric take an eight-foot section and put it out front where the land was eroding, and they had surrounded it with a variety of shrubs and flowering plants. Lucas thought the whole effect was charming and gave the place a homey look.

"It'll all come together once we put out mulch and pine straw and decorative rock," Honey told Lucas, her tone crisp and professional, "to sort of give it a finished look. It won't be completely finished, of course, until we plant trees and ever-greens and do your garden and playground. You should be hearing from the company who builds them soon." She glanced around as though trying to find something else to fix her gaze on besides his face. "Well, it's beginning to get dark. Perhaps we should call it a day. Eric, do you need a ride home?"

The blond man shook his head. "No, I'll catch a ride with one of the others," he said. "Thanks anyway."

Lucas watched as Honey walked away without even so much as a good-bye. She climbed into her truck and drove off. He was left standing next to Eric.

Lucas studied the man beneath hooded eyes. Are you tired, Severnson?" he asked.

Eric wiped the sweat from his brow with an old cloth and shook his head. "Not too bad. I think I'll go have a cold beer. That's just what I like at the end of a hard day."

Lucas nodded. "Yeah, I know what you mean." He glanced around at his yard, his pride stirred at seeing the job they'd performed. It felt good to know he'd had a hand in the work. He was tired, but it was a pleasant tiredness. He wasn't tied up in knots or mentally exhausted as he was accustomed to being at the end of a workday. He took a deep breath of the fresh country air.   Mind if I join you for that beer?" he asked.

Eric looked surprised. He hesitated. "I'm not sure you'd like the place. It's kind of . . . different. Nothing fancy like they have in Houston, mind you. A lot of guys go there after work, and you don't have to get all dressed up."

"So we can go the way we are?"

"Well, I'd like to wash my face and hands and maybe comb my hair first."

"You can use my bathroom if you like."

Eric shrugged. "Yeah, okay."

Twenty minutes later, once Eric had dismissed the workers and they'd both had a chance to clean up, they were on their way. Lucas drove his Cadillac as Eric gave directions to the bar. They pulled up in front of a single-story brick building on the outskirts of town and parked.

"I don't believe I've ever been to this place," Lucas told him. "Is it new?"

Eric nodded. "Only been here a year or so. You probably won't like it," he said once more. "I'm sure you're not used to—"

"Hey, I've seen my share of dumpy cowboy bars, if that's what you mean." Lucas climbed out of the car and followed the other man inside.

It was too dark to see much when they first entered. Lucas paused just inside the front door and tried to adjust his eyes to the lighting. The small tavern was almost empty, with the exception of a few men sitting around the bar, a couple of them wearing construction hats.

"Why don't we get a table at the back," Eric suggested, already moving in that direction. "That way we won't be disturbed."

Lucas thought the other man looked anxious, and he was certain he felt self-conscious about the place. Sure, it wasn't much to look at, but Lucas remembered a time in his not-too-distant past when he used to frequent such places. He followed Eric to a small table and sat down with his back facing the bar. The bartender appeared out of nowhere.

"I think I'll just order a coke," Lucas told Eric. "My stomach has been giving me a little trouble. Booze just aggravates the problem."

"I'll have a beer," Eric said. He waited until the bartender left to fill the order, then turned to Lucas. "So, does Honey know you have an ulcer?"

The question caught Lucas off guard. "No, and I don't want her to."

"You really got it bad for her, huh?"

Lucas nodded slowly. "Is it that obvious?"

Eric smiled. "Let me just say this. If you were in my country and you looked at a woman the way I've seen you look at Honey, you'd have to marry her."

Lucas leaned closer. "I want her back, Severnson. I want to give our relationship a second chance. I know we can make it work this time."

"Why are you telling me this?"

"Because—" Lucas paused and glanced around, finding that the bar was suddenly filling up with more men. A couple of them stood beside a vintage jukebox selecting music, and a moment later a slow number bellowed out from one of the speakers. He turned back to Eric. "I want to know what Honey means to you."

Eric pondered it. "That's a tough question, Lucas."

"Do you love her?" Lucas held his breath.

The man nodded easily. "Of course I love her. I can't think of another person in this world I'm closer to."

Lucas's heart sank. "So what are we going to do about it?"

They were interrupted when the bartender reappeared carrying their drinks. As he set them on the table, Lucas couldn't help but notice the crowd. "Well, this seems to be a real man's place." He took a sip of his drink and leaned back in his chair as a slow country song blared from the jukebox. "Now, back to this problem we have with Honey—"

Someone tapped Lucas on the shoulder, and he glanced around. A tall, slender man stood before him. "Yeah, what can I do for you?" Lucas asked.

"You wanna dance?" the man asked.

The question drew a blank from Lucas. "Dance? With who?" he asked, glancing around the room. There weren't any women present. He caught sight of two men slow-dancing in front of the jukebox and froze. "You mean with you?" he asked the stranger in disbelief. When the man nodded, Lucas chuckled under his breath. "No, man, I'm not into that sort of thing."

"Then how come you're sitting in a gay bar?" the man asked.

"Gay bar?" Lucas snapped his head around and met Eric's amused eyes. "This is a gay bar," he hissed. "Did you know that?"

"Of course I know," Eric told him matter-of-factly, "and if you won't dance with the gentleman, I will."

Lucas felt as though the world had turned upside down. "You will?" Suddenly it hit him, and he threw his head back and laughed.

Eric tensed. "What's so funny?"

Lucas slapped Eric on the back. "I'm laughing because now I realize you and I can become good friends," he said. "And as a friend, I'm going to ask you if you can help me get out of this place without being seen."

Nine

The painters Honey had called for Lucas arrived the following morning ready to go to work, picking up where he'd left off. Lucas left them and drove to the hardware store for more paint and supplies, deciding he would select wallpaper while he was there as well. After searching through several sample books, though, he realized he had no idea what to buy. In the end, he took the books home with him. Perhaps he could convince Honey to offer an opinion on the ones he liked.

Lucas almost winced. After their confrontation the day before, Honey probably wasn't even speaking to him. What made him think she would help select wallpaper for his bathroom?

He'd never expected Honey to give him so much trouble, he thought, glancing out the window at the passing scenery as he drove. Summer was quickly slipping away, he realized. Todd and Melissa would be returning to school soon. Damn, he couldn't wait to see them. He only wished he and

Honey could straighten out their problems in the meantime.

Lucas spotted a brightly colored tree from among a thicket of loblolly pines and saw that the leaves had already begun to change. It saddened him to think fall might come and go and he wouldn't be any closer to winning Honey back. He was even further saddened to realize he might have to spend the holidays alone, as he had the past three years. He wondered if he was any closer to winning her back than when he'd first arrived. He had been so certain of her love the night he'd shared her bed. Holding her in his arms tightly after their lovemaking, he'd believed in his heart that there was nothing they couldn't work out together.

Lucas drove the last mile home, deciding he would go ahead and help the painters finish his house. There was nothing else for him to do, he thought glumly. No job, no family, nothing in his life that particularly interested him. He'd never had the time to develop a hobby, and he'd never participated in sports. He seldom even watched it on television, because he'd spent most weekends working. Lucas wondered how a man could live to be thirty-five and have such an empty existence.

When Lucas pulled into his driveway a few minutes later, Honey's truck was already there, and his decision to help the painters was all but forgotten. He found her in his backyard setting up the sprinklers.

"Hi," he said, coming up to stand beside her as she did her best to straighten a twisted water hose. She was wearing those denim cutoffs again, he saw, the ones that made his blood boil.

Honey nodded, and her ponytail bobbed at the back of her head with the greeting. "Your sod looks good this morning, don't you think?"

"Yeah, great," he said, glancing around in mock interest. The last thing on his mind that morning was how his sod had fared during the night. He and Honey had wasted too much time already talking about nonessentials.

"In a couple of weeks you won't even see the seams."

Lucas would have been blind not to notice how tired she looked—her mouth drawn, dark circles shadowing the area beneath her blue eyes. She looked worried. Was it money? he wondered. He resisted the urge to take her in his arms and kiss away her troubles one by one. He would insist on paying her today for the work she and Eric had already completed.

"What's wrong, didn't you sleep well last night?" he finally asked when she yawned. He knew how to take her mind off her worries and make her sleep like a baby, he wanted to tell her.

Honey glanced up at him quickly, expecting to find some hint of amusement lurking in his eyes, but his expression was one of genuine concern. "I guess I miss the kids," she said. "I keep telling myself it's only a few more days, but—" She paused and shrugged. "I can't help it."

"Maybe you should write them a letter and tell them." He followed her to the water spigot at the side of his house. She turned it on, and the sprinklers coughed and sputtered to life.

"I write to them every day," she said. "I've never seen two weeks drag by so slowly in my life. Next time I'm going to insist they let the parents visit at least once."

Lucas nodded thoughtfully. "Yeah, time *does* go by slowly when you miss someone. Sometimes if you just try to stay busy, that helps."

His voice held such conviction that she knew he was speaking from experience. "Did it help you?"

He laughed. "Not always. Holidays are bad no matter how hard you try not to think about it." He remembered how he used to dread seeing the Christmas decorations go up every year in Houston. Of course, he always visited with Todd and Melissa on holidays, but it wasn't the same as living with them. He missed the little things that came from being a part of a family. He missed the little stick-figure drawings his children made and Honey displayed so proudly on the refrigerator. He missed the way Honey decorated for the holidays and the smells that often greeted him when he stepped inside the house after a long day.

"It was wrong of me to move so far away," Honey said as though thinking out loud.

Lucas studied the graceful arcs of water shooting out from the sprinklers, how they reflected the morning sun like tiny crystals. He shrugged. "It was only natural you'd want to return home when we separated," he pointed out.

"I honestly never thought you'd miss the kids the way you have," she said, facing him squarely for the first time since he'd arrived. "I thought—" She stopped herself abruptly. The man had never looked more desirable than he did at that moment, his face shadowed with a morning beard that her palms itched to touch. His eyes were a clear toasty brown in the sunlight, his hair a deep mahogany.

Everything feminine inside of her sprang to life as she gazed at the square jaw, the corded neck muscles, and finally, those wide shoulders. His shirt lay open at the collar, exposing enough chest hair to capture her rapt attention. "It doesn't really matter what I thought," she said at last. "It was wrong. I just didn't know what else to do at the time."

"It's not important, Honey." He could see the misery and guilt in her eyes and didn't want to prolong it. He'd stared guilt and misery in the face for three long years and was ready to move on.

"I only hope you can forgive me one day."

"There's nothing to forgive."

"Well, I suppose I'd better get started," she said, looking around his yard. "I should get most of the work finished up today. If you like, we can ride to the furniture store in Fort Worth tomorrow and pick out some things for your house."

Lucas was clearly surprised. "You mean you're going to help me?"

She laughed. She really wasn't angry anymore at his faked injury. She'd felt foolish at first, knowing he'd conjured the whole thing up so he could spend more time with her. Of course, she had been the one who'd complicated matters by inviting him into her bed, something she had trouble believing she'd done. But it had seemed right. She'd missed her children so badly and was worried about her finances. She had craved human contact. She had wanted to be held for a while, wanted to feel another's body against her own.

Honey realized now it was the single biggest mistake she'd ever made. But she had learned that by making her own decisions, she was also accountable for the mistakes that sometimes resulted.

"Well, I did think of backing out after the stunt you pulled with your foot," she finally said, "but Eric talked me out of it. He even offered to watch the store so I could get away. We don't get to take much time off because we're so tied down."

If Lucas was disappointed that her decision had been made because of Eric's suggestions, he didn't show it. He was learning to take what he could get from Honey, only what she was willing to give. "Then, why don't we make a day of it?" he asked. "I'll even take you someplace nice for lunch. Maybe to a Mexican restaurant." When she started to protest, he stopped her. "It's the least I can do, Honey, since you're giving up a day's work. Unless, of course, you'd rather I pay you," he added quickly.

"Of course I don't want payment," she said, indignant that he would even suggest it. "We can plan to leave around eight o'clock tomorrow morning, if that's okay with you. It won't take us more than an hour to get there. I think you'll find a better selection in the stores in Fort Worth." She started back to the front of his house as though having dismissed him, but he followed.

"You don't mind if I help you with the yard today, do you?" When she looked doubtful, he went on. "The house smells like a paint factory right now, and I don't want to get in the way. Besides, I enjoyed working out here yesterday."

Honey pondered it a moment. She knew if Lucas didn't stay busy, he would bug her to death. The best thing she could do was give him enough work so he wouldn't have time to bother her. She finally relented. "Okay, but please try not to hurt your-self."

She looked so serious, he couldn't help grinning. "If I do, would you promise to nurse me the way you did the other day?" he teased.

She didn't looked amused. "No. If you hurt yourself this time, you're on your own."

By lunchtime, Lucas had planted a good number of evergreens near his driveway, working alongside a couple of college boys Honey sometimes called on when she was in a bind. Lucas prided himself on the fact that he was able to keep up with the boys, who were at least sixteen years his junior. At noon, they carried their lunch sacks to the shade of a giant live oak, and Lucas invited Honey inside, where he made sandwiches. The painters had driven into town for lunch, promising to be back before long.

"It's really taking shape out there," Lucas said, peering out the window at the lot they'd spent so much time working. "I never thought it would look so good."

"I'm pleased with it," Honey said. "Once we're finished, I'll set up a maintenance plan with you. We can care for it ourselves or instruct you on how to keep it healthy and in shape. You certainly don't want to neglect it once you've spent all this money."

Lucas thought about what she'd said. He'd ne-glected his marriage and watched it die right under his nose. "You're right," he said, agreeing so vehemently that Honey was certain they were talk-ing about two different things.

Honey smiled. "I hear you bought Vera's old car."

Lucas grimaced at the memory. "Yeah, the stubborn old woman really put the screws to me."

Honey chuckled softly. "Well, I don't know what you paid for it, but any amount would have been too much. She's going out this afternoon to shop for a new one."

"I hope she ends up with a lemon," he said. "And I hope it breaks down on some back country road, and I'm the only motorist who comes along."

Honey slapped his arm playfully. "Oh, Lucas, you're awful." Her look sobered. "You really would give her a ride, though, wouldn't you? I mean, the woman has been like a mother to me."

His eyes softened. "I'd do it for you."

Honey didn't quite know how to respond, and it took every ounce of self-control she could muster to force her gaze away from his. She couldn't look into his eyes without losing herself, couldn't look at that ruggedly handsome face without wanting to touch it and trace the firm lines of his jaw. Her thoughts automatically strayed to the night they'd spent together in each other's arms, how he'd felt against her—big and warm and strong. She knew his scent as well as she knew her own. She was equally familiar with his body, but that didn't prevent her from wanting to discover more.

She stood. "I'd better get back to work."

Lucas stood as well and walked toward her with the ease and grace of a large jungle cat. "It always happens between us, doesn't it, Honey?" he said, his voice dropping an octave. He didn't have to be able to read her mind to know she'd been thinking of that night together in her bed. "We can't sit together five minutes without thinking about that night. And other nights," he added softly. "And all the nights to come."

"Lucas, please—" She gave an embarrassed laugh and raised one hand as though to silence him. He closed the distance between them and halted only inches from her, but he didn't reach out for her as she had expected. He didn't have to. She could feel the heat emanating from his body, and he caressed her face with his eyes so thoroughly, it was as if he'd actually reached out and stroked her cheek with his fingers. It would have been less unnerving, she realized, had he simply taken her in his arms. As it was, not knowing what his next move would be, she felt vulnerable and exposed.

"Why do you keep fighting me, Honey?" he asked, offering her a tender smile. It was the kind of smile a benevolent father might offer a mischievous child. "Surely you're not playing hard to get after all we've been through together."

His voice, like liquid velvet, coaxed a warmth to her lower belly that hadn't been there before. Her limbs felt heavy and lethargic, her weight suddenly too much for her own knees to bear. "I don't play games, Lucas," she said.

"No?" He tilted his head to one side. "Sometimes I can't help but wonder."

Lucas arrived at Honey's the following morning shortly before eight o'clock and found her ready, wearing neatly pressed jeans and a brick-red shirt with padded shoulders that heightened the color in her cheeks. Her long hair had been pulled back in a single thick braid, interwoven with a ribbon that matched her shirt. Lucas smiled broadly at the sight as he followed her from her front porch to his car, taking a moment to enjoy both her hair and her lovely swaying hips, which looked so delectable in her denims. His smile faded, however, when he joined her in the front seat and noted her troubled look.

"Why so glum?" he asked as he folded the map he'd been studying earlier and stashed it in the glove compartment. He planned to take the back roads to Fort Worth, thinking the country scenery would offer more visual appeal than the interstate. In the past he would never have considered it. He would have taken the quickest route from point A to point B, never taking the time to discover what lay between. Of course, he had selfish reasons for taking the back way, he knew. The back way was longer. It meant spending more time with Honey.

"I'm worried about Vera," Honey said at last. "Her arthritis is giving her a fit this morning."

He arched one brow. "Do you think it's wise to leave her? I could always shop for furniture another day." He was making the supreme sacrifice, since he'd thought of little else but spending the day with her. But he knew she would not enjoy herself if she was worried about her housekeeper.

"Oh, she should be okay," Honey said after thinking it over. "I told her to rest today. She's getting too old to carry the work load around here. It hasn't been as bad with Todd and Melissa gone, but when they get back, she'll have her hands full once more."

"What are you going to do?"

"Well, it's obvious I'm going to have to hire someone to help out. First of all, I don't have time to take care of the house the way I should. And the kids need someone at home for them after school. Vera has been more like a grandmother than a housekeeper." She sighed and leaned her head back against the seat. "I don't know what I'd do without her."

"You'd get by, Honey. You've been handling problems for longer than you know."

"What do you mean?" she asked.

Lucas continued to look straight ahead as he drove down the long tree-lined driveway and turned onto the main road. "You keep telling me how you never once made a decision for yourself, but that's not true. You lost your mother at an early age, and you managed to put that behind you when it would have traumatized most kids." He remembered how bad it had been for him when he'd lost his own mother. True, she had abandoned the family, but he'd missed her just the same and had carried a chip on his shoulder for a long time.

"You more or less ran the household afterward, from what I understand," he went on, "a job that would have intimidated most folks. You were planning dinner parties and special events before most girls your age were allowed to wear lipstick."

"Well, Vera helped," she pointed out, but Honey knew it was true. She had been forced to take over a lot of the domestic duties at an early age. She'd known how to select a good wine by the time she was twelve years old, knew which wine best complemented a certain dish. She knew how to plan and set a nice table and where to seat her father's guests once they arrived to insure a party's success. She'd known how to converse intelligently with his guests, how to steer the conversation away from sensitive areas, how to deal with those who drank too much. Unfortunately, there hadn't been much of a need for those skills when she'd been forced to earn a living.

"Sometimes I think that's why Major tried to do all your thinking for you," Lucas said, interrupting her musings. "I think he wanted you to feel dependent on him so you wouldn't leave."

"I don't know what you mean."

"I believe Major needed you more than you ever needed him, Honey. He needed you there to do all those things that his wife wasn't capable of doing for him. He prevented you from attending that architectural school, not because he didn't think you could do the work, but because it was so far from home. He wanted you home on holidays and in the summer to run the house. And that's one of the reasons he acted so indignant about your having a career. He wanted you around for his own needs." Lucas glanced at her and was surprised by the stricken look on her face. "I'm sorry, Honey, I shouldn't have said any of that. I probably don't know what I'm talking about."

Honey twisted around in the seat so that she was facing him. "I believe you're right, Lucas," she said, "but for the life of me I never saw it that way until now. I never thought for a minute that Major needed me." And she hadn't. It was as though she were suddenly seeing her life and relationship with her father for the first time.

Lucas shrugged. "Major and I were a lot alike, you know. I think that's why the old buzzard and I knocked heads so often. Needless to say, we made the same mistakes. We both drove you away because we needed you so desperately in our lives. We never gave much thought to what you wanted or needed."

"I never thought you needed anybody."

"I tried to hide it. Even from myself." He offered her a slight smile. "It took me a while to come to terms with that fact, of course. It sort of blew my macho image all to hell."

Honey turned and gazed out the window for a moment, not wanting Lucas to know how close to tears she was at his simple declaration. "You made a lot of money for my father, didn't you?" she said after a moment.

He nodded. "He did all right. We both did."

"Was it illegal?"

"Not illegal, just . . ." He paused in thought. "Maybe a bit opportunistic. I overheard information about the distribution center long before it became a reality. Actually, Major and I made it a reality. But because I was a licensed realtor at the time and had to get around conflict-of-interest laws, I had to find someone else to move on it for me. Someone who had power and money. Major Buchannan," he added. "I merely stood in the shadows and planned our strategy while Major acted on it. We made a good team for a while. I had the information and real estate knowledge, Major had the money and clout. He pulled a lot of strings."

"You could have gotten into trouble, though," she said.

"I could have lost my license, if that's what you mean." He glanced at her, wondering if she was shocked. Her expression was unreadable.

"You said you and Major made a good team. What changed that?"

Lucas looked directly at her. "You did. Major came down on me hard when he realized I was after you."

"Why?"

"He didn't think I was good enough." Lucas's upper lip curled almost scornfully. "I was good enough to fatten his bank account, but not good enough to share his daughter's bed." He grinned. "Of course, that didn't stop me, and the rest is history."

"Would you take such a chance again?" she asked. "I mean, knowing that it's wrong, would you risk your career for the sake of money?"

So she did have an opinion on what he'd done, Lucas thought. At the same time, she didn't sound judgmental or shocked or disappointed or any of those things he would have expected. He pondered her question. "I'd like to think I wouldn't. I know what I did was wrong, and there have been times when I've regretted it. I've wondered if maybe I might have been just as successful had I played strictly by the rules. But would I do it again?" He sighed. "I probably would if I was up against a wall. If it meant feeding my family."

Honey thought about all he'd said. "You once told me you owned me, that you'd paid for me by making my daddy a richer man."

Lucas felt as though he'd swallowed a piece of hot coal. He looked at her and saw the memory was as painful for her as when he'd said it, and he watched the color drain from her face.

"I was drunk out of my mind that night, Honey. I think, if you'll remember, we were celebrating my biggest sale ever and—" He shook his head. "I have no excuse. I was drunk and full of myself. I apologized the next day, and I'll apologize again if it'll help. We both know that human beings can't be bought."

"Did you know it then?"

"No. I really did feel as thought I owned you. I suppose that's why I was so devastated when you left and even more so when I discovered I couldn't throw you over my shoulder and take you back home the way I wanted." He offered her a wry smile. "As you must know, there are laws to protect people like you from people like me."

"Do you feel you still own me, Lucas?"

He faced the road once again, swerving the car gently to one side to miss a pothole. "No." A muscle ticked in his jaw, and Honey realized it was a question that stirred his deepest emotions. "I feel as if you belong to me as far as our hearts are concerned, but realistically I know there's not a damn thing I can do to get you back against your will." After a moment, he added, "And there are times when I tell myself you may never come back. So, I try to be patient a while longer and . . ." He paused. "And then I think of ways to carry on in case you decide not to return."

He glanced out the window, not wanting her to see the raw pain in his eyes. While he would not and could not *force* Honey back into his life, neither would he have her return out of sheer pity. That's why he hadn't told her of his ulcer and probably never would. He'd lost a lot in three years, and it had brought him to his knees emotionally. But there was a vestige of pride inside that he would not give up. He could be humbled, but not stripped of his dignity.

Honey was touched to the core by his revelation. Never before had Lucas opened himself up so, never before had he exposed himself with such honesty and clarity. She felt her heart swell with emotion. "Oh, Lucas." She reached over and covered one of his hands on the steering wheel. Their gazes met and locked and suddenly the only sound they heard was the combined beating of their hearts. Lucas took her hand in his palm, then raised it to his lips for a kiss. He closed his eyes briefly, feeling closer to Honey at that moment than at any time in their marriage.

Honey felt her heart would surely burst at the tender sight. That one simple act was sweeter than anything she'd ever seen him do, sweeter even than the first time he'd held Todd and Melissa in his arms and thanked her for them. The act was sweeter still because he'd given of himself, given her something that could be stored inside her heart for all eternity, something that never had to be shared or given away.

"You know what I wish?" she said, fixing him with a soft gaze.

"What? What do you wish?" he asked, his voice so tender it inspired confidence. He squeezed her hand.

She smiled, almost shyly. "That we could make love."

Ten

The blood drained from Lucas's face, and he almost ran off the road. He dropped her hand suddenly and turned his attention back to his driving. Once he'd righted the situation, he looked at her, and his voice was earnest when he spoke. "We can, baby, we can."

A few minutes later, Lucas pulled off the main road onto a gravel one that was flanked on both sides by tall loblolly pines. They traveled a short distance before he found a dirt road, nothing more than a path, really, where the trees grew thicker and made passage difficult. He waited until they were well out of sight before he parked beneath a tall oak and cut the engine.

Lucas reached for her, and Honey came willingly into his arms. His lips touched hers, and they both shivered, knowing that the hours of holding back made the union even sweeter. Lucas touched her face and hair and ran his fingers down her throat before he undid the small pewter buttons on her blouse.

162

When her blouse and bra lay on the seat beside them, Lucas buried his face against her breasts and inhaled her scent. Honey sighed, leaned her head back against the seat, and gave in to the sheer pleasure of his lovemaking. When he reached for the fastening on her jeans, she was only too happy to assist.

"Lucas," she said with a moan when his fingers located the very apex of her desire. "Oh, Lucas, I really do want you. But you know that, don't you? You've always known that."

He nodded, and with his help she freed him from his own clothing. When they faced each other once again, they were completely naked. "I've never made love in a car before," she confessed.

"I'm glad you told me that," he said, smiling as he kissed her. She looked ethereal, not of this world, with the sun spilling across her bare breasts and stomach. He raised his head briefly, and his brown eyes teased her. "I've never made love to you in a car before, so if you had said otherwise, I would naturally have had questions."

She laughed softly, then kissed him, thinking no man on earth should have a right to taste so good, so *right*. She was tempted to ask if he had made love to others in the front seat of his car or perhaps taken someone to his bed, especially during the past three years, but she didn't. She had no right. She would take comfort in knowing that, while he may have given himself physically to another woman, she still had claim to his heart.

When Lucas positioned her over that part of his body that she'd stroked to hardness only a moment before, she sank onto him slowly and cried out in pleasure. Their mouths and tongues reunited as their bodies rocked gently to and fro on the front seat, and later they shuddered in each other's arms and captured the sounds of their release with their lips.

The trip to Fort Worth was a success, and they celebrated Lucas's furniture bargains over a plate of spicy Mexican food before heading back home. "I like everything you chose," Honey said once they'd climbed into his car, completely sated now that she'd eaten everything on her plate and part of Lucas's meal as well.

Lucas laughed. "What do you mean, *I* chose? As I recall, you picked out everything yourself."

"Well, you said you wanted my help," she said in her own defense.

"I think Todd and Melissa will approve of their new bedroom suites," he said, "but I want them to pick out bedspreads and curtains for their rooms."

"Make sure they choose something bright," Honey told him, "and that the curtains won't block out the sun."

His gaze met hers, and he read the silent message there. "I will," he promised.

They chatted easily as the car ate up the miles toward home. When Honey began talking about her landscaping business, Lucas decided it was time to talk about what had been on his mind since the night before.

"I've been wanting to discuss your business with you," he said.

"Discuss it in what way?" Honey truly felt comfortable with him now as she leaned back in the seat. She could not remember enjoying a time with him as she had that day. Their lovemaking that morning had set the tone for intimacy, and several times during the afternoon, Lucas had taken her hand in his and squeezed it, his dark eyes saying more than words. There would be time for doubts and recriminations later, but for the moment she would simply enjoy it.

"I think Eric misses Sweden."

She couldn't imagine what that had to do with her business per se, but she nodded. "Yes, he misses it very much."

"Does his gay lifestyle have anything to do with his reasons for leaving?"

Honey raised cautious eyes to his. "How did you find out?"

"I had a beer with him the other night at the place where he hangs out."

"And what did you do when you found out?"

"Well, I left early, of course. I didn't see any reason to stay, since I wasn't in the mood for dancing."

Honey laughed, and he wondered if she knew how sexy the sound was, slightly husky but musical enough to be quite feminine. "I hope you didn't say anything to hurt Eric's feelings," she said.

"Don't take me for such a jerk, Honey. I couldn't care less about the guy's sexual preferences." To himself he added silently, *As long as those preferences don't include my wife.* But he didn't voice the thought aloud, and he wasn't about to confess how relieved he'd been to discover Eric posed no threat to him where Honey was concerned. She could already list his faults in alphabetical order, he wasn't about to add to the list.

"The real tragedy here isn't that he's gay," Lucas

went on. "It's the fact he can't level with his family. Otherwise, I think the guy would be on the next plane home."

Honey nodded in agreement. She knew if Eric had the funds, he would probably return home. He'd never been truly happy in the States, and sometimes she felt guilty because she was certain he'd remained because of her and the business. They had met shortly after her divorce at a flower show while studying a particularly beautiful and exotic plant. They'd met when they both desperately needed a friend, and even though Honey hadn't known he was gay at the time, she had sensed his sincerity. He'd never come on to her. Later, as time passed and they'd discovered their mutual interests lay in gardening, they began to toss around the idea of starting a business. Yet even though she knew Eric loved the landscaping business, she suspected he would be happier owning one in Sweden. But she could not afford to buy his share herself, and she knew Eric would never just sell out and abandon her.

She hoped in time Eric would be happier and accept who and what he was, just as she had accepted it when he'd told her. She was certain that if given the chance, his family would understand. But she really didn't feel comfortable discussing Eric's personal life or their business arrangement with Lucas or anybody else.

"I'm glad we agree about Eric," she said, "and that you accept him for who he is. But I don't see what this has to do with the business."

Lucas didn't know any other way to say it, so he blurted it out. "I'd like to try to buy him out, Honey."

She didn't answer right away, but then she didn't have to. Her feelings were quite clear by the glassy look that stole into her eyes. Her body became ramrod stiff, and her eyes glittered like blue diamonds when she met his gaze.

"You're kidding, of course." It was not a question, it was a statement, and the tone of her voice dared him to suggest otherwise.

Lucas realized he had stepped into hostile territory, and he wondered for a moment if she had any idea how much she resembled her father when she was angry. "Look, before you get all bent out of shape, let me say this. I could turn that place into a gold mine."

Her voice was as dull and flat as the gray road in front of them when she spoke. "What do you know of landscaping, Lucas?"

"I don't know a damn thing—"

"Exactly."

"But I know it has to do with people and selling a product. There's not much I *don't* know about that," he added. When she didn't respond, he went on. "You and Eric have done an excellent job providing the product. Why not let somebody like me take the ball and go with it?"

Honey leveled her gaze at him. "Oh, I'll tell you where you can go with it, all right."

Her attitude surprised him, and for a moment he drove in silence. "Why won't you even listen to what I have to say?" he asked once he'd turned into the drive leading to her house. "Why won't you at least let me help you?"

She twisted around in the seat and faced him squarely. "Because you could never simply help me, Lucas. You'd have to show me *your* way of doing things. The decisions would be *your* decisions. In the end, I wouldn't even recognize the place. It would be *your* dream, Lucas, not mine."

"I could be a silent partner," he said as he pulled in front of the house and parked.

She laughed hollowly. "You've never been silent about anything in your life."

His jaw muscle was working overtime as he stared out the window, trying to get himself under control. He had never seen this side of Honey before, and he almost didn't recognize her. "You'd be surprised how I can hold my tongue if I have to," he muttered.

"What's that supposed to mean?"

Lucas faced her, and their gazes locked, doing silent battle with each other. It was hard to believe she was the same woman he'd spent the day with, had made love to in the front seat only a few hours before.

"Meaning I've kept my mouth shut about Melissa," he said tersely, "once I thought it over. I don't agree with your taking her to a psychologist, but I've decided to back you nevertheless, because I know you wouldn't do it without giving it serious thought. And I've kept my mouth shut about other things as well. Your money problems, for instance." Her eyes widened like saucers the minute the words left his mouth.

"That's right, Honey, I know you're broke. Busted. And as much as it killed me when I found out, I never once offered to help you." He leaned close. "That's not easy, Honey, knowing that your family may be doing without. If I was the bastard you make me out to be, I would have already dragged you into court and taken the kids away from you so I could make sure they had enough."

Honey was speechless. "Are you accusing me of neglecting our children?" she demanded.

"I'm accusing you of being so damn proud, you can't make yourself come to me for help."

"Todd and Melissa have never wanted for anything. I'm perfectly capable of caring for them!"

"How? You've used up all your trust."

Honey's mouth dropped open. "H-how did you know about that?"

Lucas realized he'd said more than he should. "I overheard it the first day I drove out to your office."

"You were spying on me!"

"No. It was an accident."

"Funny how you're always overhearing conversations, isn't it, Lucas? First the distribution center and now—"

"That's enough!" he shouted, making them both jump. "Listen, Honey, I've come completely clean with you. If I've made mistakes in my life, both personally and professionally, I'm sorry. I'm sorry!" he repeated a bit louder. Honey grabbed the door handle, but he stopped her. "Just hear me out," he ordered.

Honey released the handle. She crossed her arms and waited. "Go ahead, Lucas. Give it your best shot."

Lucas raked one hand over his face and realized he was perspiring heavily. "Honey, I can't go back and change the past. As much as I'd like to," he added. "But I've paid for my mistakes more than you'll ever know. I made money on that distribution center and got a new start in life, but it wasn't worth all the sucking up I had to do to your old man."

"My father is dead," she said between clenched teeth. "Can't we leave him out of this?"

"Okay," he agreed, nodding. "So that just leaves us with the problem of what to do with our relationship."

"We have no relationship."

"But we could if we worked at it."

"We?"

"It all boils down to give and take, Honey. Now, I'm willing to give, but only to an extent."

Her mouth fell open. "What are you saying?"

Lucas hitched his chin upward, realizing he could make or break whatever it was they had between them at the moment. "I'm willing to make up for my mistakes to you and the kids, Honey, but I'm not going to hang from my heels for the rest of my life. I want to start with a clean slate. And I'm willing to meet you halfway. In return, I expect *you* to meet *me* halfway. I'm agreeable to all these things you want in life for yourself, but I expect you to share in my life as well." He paused. "One more thing—"

"What?" Her bottom lip trembled.

"Don't take my acquiescence as a sign of weakness. I *can* be pushed too far, you know."

She met his steady gaze even as she sought blindly for the door handle. He had delivered an ultimatum, which meant, of course, his patience had run out. He was prepared to risk it all. "I think I'll pass," she said. She grabbed the handle and jerked it hard, then pushed the door wide open. She didn't even bother to close it behind her as she ran to the house.

Lucas watched her go, and his world shattered around him.

Three days later, Honey awoke with the sun shining in her face. She opened her eyes and found Vera standing beside the tall windows where the heavy draperies had been tied back with what looked like pieces of rope. Honey rubbed her eyes and sat up. "What are you doing?" she asked, noting the way the sun slanted across the antique Persian rug. Dust motes sparkled like gold dust along the shafts of sunlight.

"I'm trying to let the sun in," Vera said matter-of-factly. "Don't you think it's about time?"

In answer, Honey fell back onto the bed limply. "Oh, Vera, just leave me alone this morning. I'm too tired."

"That's what you said yesterday. And the day before." Vera stepped closer to the bed. "Eric has called twice. He's worried about you."

Honey pulled the covers to her chin and turned over so Vera couldn't see the rush of tears. "Tell him I have a virus, and I'll be in tomorrow."

Vera didn't answer immediately, and a moment later she rounded the bed and sank onto it next to Honey. "No," she said. "I'm not going to do that." Honey opened her eyes in question. "That's how it began with your mother," Vera said. "She didn't want to get out of bed either."

Honey gritted her teeth. "I'm not like my mother."

Vera went on as though she hadn't heard her. "First she started sleeping late in the morning and missing appointments, so I would call and cancel them for her. Then she didn't feel like meeting friends. After that she refused to go even to the hairdresser." Vera shook her head sadly. "Before long, she didn't want to come down for meals, so I brought trays up here."

Honey sniffed, but the tears came anyway. "My mother was weak."

"Your mother was miserable and unhappy, dear, and had no idea what to do about it. I tried to convince her to work out her problems with your father or leave, but the thought of doing either frightened her. I think it was easier for her to stay locked in her room than have to make those decisions."

Honey swiped angrily at her tears. "She allowed my father to run all over her. She paved the road for him to run all over me."

"Yes, but he didn't do it for very long, did he? As soon as you were old enough, you took off."

"And married a man just like him."

"Maybe you're attracted to strong men, have you ever thought of that?" Vera didn't wait for her to answer. "Maybe it's because you're such a strong woman." Vera tucked an errant strand of hair behind Honey's ear and smiled. "You're right. You're nothing like your mother. But please don't remember her weaknesses. Try to have compassion when you think of her."

Honey nodded. "I will." After a moment, she added, "I think I've always secretly worried I would be like her, you know?" When the other woman smiled knowingly, she went on. "I don't know why, though. My mother didn't raise me, Vera, you did. And you're one of the strongest, bravest women I've ever known."

Vera chuckled and wiped one of Honey's tears with the corner of her apron. "That's why I don't think you'd be happy with a man you could lead around by the nose, dear. You need someone as strong willed and determined and stubborn as you are."

Honey blinked. "What are you trying to say?"

"Don't choose unhappiness when there is so much pleasure to be found in this old world."

The two women embraced for a moment, and Honey snuggled against Vera, remembering how she'd done so so many times before. "I love you, Vera," she whispered. "You've always been there for me, and I will never forget it."

"There's somebody else out there who wants very much to be there for you," Vera said gently.

Honey raised her eyes. "You mean Lucas?" She chuckled. "I thought you hated Lucas."

"I've never hated him, though I think he's somewhat of a rascal. But he's a good-hearted rascal, and I know he'll take care of you and the children as long as he has breath in him. And I know you love that man more than you'll ever love anyone else. That's good enough for me." She paused. "'Course that probably doesn't matter now that he's gone."

Honey shot her an anxious look. "What do you mean, gone?"

"I reckon he went back to Houston. I've been by his house twice to give him the bill of sale for my car, but he was nowhere to be found."

Honey didn't waste another second. She threw off the bed covers. "He'd damn sure better not be gone!" she said, running to her closet.

Vera chuckled. "You didn't expect him to wait around forever, did you?"

Honey tossed her another worried look. "Well, I didn't expect him to take off without a word. Besides, Todd and Melissa are arriving today," she added confidently. "I can't imagine him not being around for that." She opened her closet door and pulled out a yellow cotton dress, her mind racing ahead. "Vera, please call Eric and tell him I'd like to meet with him in the office in an hour."

"I thought you were tired and had a virus."

Honey waved the matter aside. "I'm better now." She hurried into the bathroom and closed the door. Vera chuckled under her breath as she left the room.

Lucas checked his wristwatch again as he turned off the main road and drove down the gravel one leading to his house. He was exhausted after his two-day stint in Houston, during which he'd poured over contracts and legal documents. All he could think of at the moment was a hot shower. Still, he was pleased with the results of his trip. It looked as though his attorney had located a qualified buyer for his business, and the initial offer had been fair. They would know more in a couple of weeks.

Maybe he'd sit on the front porch and relax before he drove to the church later to meet his children, who would be arriving by bus. His stomach churned excitedly. In a few days, they would have a playground area to entertain them, but until then he would spend time getting to know his son and daughter again.

He thought of Honey. Honey, who was never far from his memory and whose angry face he'd seen every time he'd closed his eyes since their argument. He squared his shoulders as he drove. He would get past all that somehow,˙ he promised himself. One day he would be able to think of her without running the full gamut of emotions. One day he would be over her. Then he saw her truck as he pulled into his driveway, and those promises vanished into thin air.

She was wearing a yellow dress, he saw, as he parked his car beside her truck and climbed out, his jacket hooked over an index finger. She'd been wearing yellow the first time he saw her, and she looked as good as she had then. She didn't budge as he approached the porch. She sat in an old rocker, watching him with blue eyes that always made his heart beat a little faster when he looked into them. Her long legs were crossed at the knees, he noticed. Just as he noticed the braids in her hair, and the yellow ribbons that had been woven in so nicely. But then he'd decided to stop noticing things like that about her, simply because it was so hard on him physically and emotionally. He needed to get tough with himself, he thought, harden himself against these things so that one day he could look at her without falling apart inside.

Honey stared wordlessly as Lucas came to a halt at the bottom step, his coat slung carelessly over one shoulder. His shirtsleeves had been rolled up to his elbows, offering a nice view of his lean forearms. His paisley tie had been loosened, his collar unbuttoned at the top, exposing just enough chest hair to tease and fascinate her imagination.

He stood with one hip thrust outward as he gazed at her, his head cocked to one side questioningly.

"Pretty fancy duds to be doing yard work in," he said, his voice unusually flat. His look was as sober as an old-maid schoolteacher's, she thought.

Honey uncurled herself slowly from the rocker and walked to the top step so that he could not help but see her long legs. And he was looking, she thought smugly, though he was trying like the devil not to. She leaned against one of the small columns and trailed her fingertips along the painted wood. Lucas's gaze followed her movements.

"I didn't come out here to work on your yard," she drawled seductively. "I came out here to work on you."

Lucas's gaze snapped upward and collided with hers, and her meaning was clear. He swallowed, and his Adam's apple bobbed along his throat. Beads of perspiration popped out on his upper lip as he studied the woman before him, who looked fresh and cool in the sultry afternoon heat. Her eyes sparkled mischievously as she continued to stroke the column beside her suggestively, and Lucas could almost feel the sensation in the pit of his stomach. She leaned closer, rubbing against the column as a cat would a chair leg, and Lucas realized suddenly that she was teasing him. The blue-eyed witch was trying to seduce him, he thought.

He took the stairs slowly, one at a time. His gaze was on her face, but he was still very much aware of the caressing motions her hands performed on that poor helpless column of wood. Each gentle stroke tightened the coil of anticipation in his gut.

When he reached the top step, he closed the distance between them, standing so close, he could see the tiny gold specks in her eyes, so close, he could count the tiny caramel-colored freckles on her nose. His thigh brushed against hers.

"Work on me?" he asked, his husky voice amused. "I didn't know I needed fixing."

Her lips curled at the corners in a coy smile. "You're right," she said after a moment. "I think you're real fine just the way you are. In fact, I don't think it gets any better." As she spoke, she tucked one knee between his so that there was no doubt what she was talking about.

Lucas sucked his breath in sharply and wiped his sweaty forehead with the back of his hand. "What's going on here, Honey?" he demanded. "Last time I saw you, you acted as though you never wanted to lay eyes on me again. You accused me of trying to run your life and make your decisions and . . ." He paused and tried to remember everything she *had* accused him of, but it was difficult to concentrate when she began a gentle sawing motion with her knee. The gentle friction warmed his belly.

Her eyes softened. "Yes, I did, didn't I?" When he nodded gravely, she went on. "But then I got to thinking about your offer."

"Offer?"

She nodded. "How you offered to meet me halfway," she said. "That's really all I ask of you, Lucas." Her voice was soothing and gentle as she reached for his tie and fingered the tiny filigree designs embedded in the silk. She inched her fingers upward and grasped the small knot at the top, then tugged gently and stood on tiptoe for a kiss. Their lips and tongues mated.

Lucas was the first to pull away. He gazed at her through cautious eyes. "Does this mean you'll marry me again?"

"Yes."

"And live where?"

"We can live here, if you like."

"What about your house? And Vera?"

"She can stay in the house until I decide what to do with it. Who knows, I may end up selling the place after all. It's too dark and gloomy to raise a family in. Or maybe I'll just donate it to a good cause." She promised herself to give it more thought later. "And Vera will be provided for. My father saw to that a long time ago when he set up my own trust. She and I were protected even when he lost everything. I like to think it was his way of showing he truly cared about us after all."

"Yes, but—"

"And we'll work out everything else that comes up in the meantime, Lucas," she assured him. "I've already talked to Eric, and he's agreeable to selling his share of the business, if you and I can come to terms. But first we'll help him with his problems, because he's my good friend and I care about him. And then we'll discuss Melissa's problems, and together I think we'll come up with a solution. And when all that's settled, we'll build that garden out back so we can rest." She chuckled. "I think we should do it together so when we grow old, we'll remember what we had to go through to get to that point. Any more questions?"

Lucas grinned. "You think you've got it all figured out, don't you?"

Her own grin was enough to tease his socks off. "I keep telling you, I'm one savvy lady."

His grin broadened. "And what am I?"

"You're one tough guy. But I'm going to change all that. I'm going to perform a regular meltdown on that heart of yours."

"You already have." He kissed her tenderly. "It's going to be better this time," he promised when he broke the kiss. "From this moment on, I want you to know that I'll always be behind you. I'll never try to control you again. I like the new you. No, I love it," he amended.

"And I love you, Lucas. I never stopped." They fell into each other's arms and held on tight, neither of them wanting to let go or risk losing the other again. After a moment, Honey looked up into his face. "Lucas, there may be times when I want you to exert a little control over me," she said somewhat shyly. "There are times I enjoy feeling vulnerable and—" She blushed. "You know."

The smile he offered her was almost brazen as he clamped her knee tightly between his own two. She didn't have to spell out her message to him. "And there will be times I'll *want* to take control," he said. "I don't mind telling you I sometimes enjoy feeling like the mighty conqueror between the sheets." He laughed. "It's an ego thing, what can I say?"

"I like ego things."

"That doesn't mean I won't expect a few counterattacks from you now and then."

"Maybe if we practice a bit," she suggested.

"I understand the new furniture was delivered yesterday while I was away. We could always break in the new mattress."

She glanced at her wristwatch. "As I see it, we have just enough time before we have to meet our children."

His children. Lucas's heart swelled at the thought. He would see his children in a few hours. But first he would make love to his wife, knowing that she was his once again and forever, knowing this time he would get it right. He linked his fingers through hers, and together they crossed the porch, side by side. Side by side, he thought, gazing down at her in sheer adoration and finding that same look mirrored in her own eyes. Everything was just as it should be.

THE EDITOR'S CORNER

Nothing could possibly put you in more of a carefree, summertime mood than the six LOVESWEPTs we have for you next month. Touching, tender, packed with emotion and wonderfully happy endings, our six upcoming romances are real treasures.

The first of these priceless stories is SARAH'S SIN by Tami Hoag, LOVESWEPT #480, a heart-grabbing tale that throbs with all the ecstasy and uncertainty of forbidden love. When hero Dr. Matt Thorne is injured, he finds himself recuperating in his sister's country inn—with a beautiful, untouched Amish woman as his nurse. Sarah Troyer's innocence and sweetness make the world seem suddenly new for this world-weary Romeo, and he woos her with his masterful bedside manner. The brash ladies' man with the bad-boy grin is Sarah's romantic fantasy come true, but there's a high price to pay for giving herself to one outside the Amish world. You'll cry and cheer for these two memorable characters as they risk everything for love. A marvelous LOVESWEPT from a very gifted author.

From our very own Iris Johansen comes a LOVESWEPT that will drive you wild with excitement—A TOUGH MAN TO TAME, #481. Hero Louis Benoit is a tiger of the financial world, and Mariana Sandell knows the danger of breaching the privacy of his lair to appear before him. Fate has sent her from Sedikhan, the glorious setting of many of Iris's previous books, to seek out Louis and make him a proposition. He's tempted, but more by the mysterious lady herself than her business offer. The secret terror in her eyes arouses his tender, protective instincts, and he vows to move heaven and earth to fend off danger . . . and keep her by his side. This grand love story will leave you breathless. Another keeper from Iris Johansen.

IN THE STILL OF THE NIGHT by Terry Lawrence, LOVESWEPT #482, proves beyond a doubt that nothing could be more romantic than a sultry southern evening. Attorney Brad Lavalier certainly finds it so, especially when he's stealing a hundred steamy kisses from Carolina Palmette. A heartbreaking scandal drove this proud beauty from her Louisiana hometown years before, and now she's back to settle her grandmother's affairs. Though she's stopped believing in the magic of love, working with devilishly sexy Brad awakens a long-denied hunger within her. And only he can slay the dragons of her past and melt her resistance to a searing attraction. Sizzling passion and deep emotion—an unbeatable combination for a marvelous read from Terry Lawrence.

Summer heat is warming you now, but your temperature will rise even higher with ever-popular Fayrene Preston's newest LOVESWEPT, FIRE WITHIN FIRE, #483. Meet powerful businessman Damien Averone, brooding, enigmatic—and burning with need for Ginnie Summers. This alluring woman bewitched him from the moment he saw her on the beach at sunrise, then stoked the flame of his desire with the entrancing music of her guitar on moonlit nights. Only sensual surrender will soothe his fiery ache for the elusive siren. But Ginnie knows the expectations that come with deep attachment, and Damien's demanding intensity is overwhelming. Together these tempestuous lovers create an inferno of passion that will sweep you away. Make sure you have a cool drink handy when you read this one because it is hot, hot, hot!

Please give a big and rousing welcome to brand-new author Cindy Gerard and her first LOVESWEPT—MAVERICK, #484, an explosive novel that will give you a charge. Hero Jesse Kincannon is one dynamite package of rugged masculinity, sex appeal, and renegade ways you can't resist. When he returns to the Flying K Ranch and fixes his smoldering gaze on Amanda Carter, he makes her his own, just as he did years before when she'd been the foreman's young daughter and he was the boss's son. Amanda owns half the ranch now, and Jesse's sudden reappearance is suspicious. However, his outlaw kisses soon convince her that he's after her heart. A riveting romance from one of our New Faces of '91! Don't miss this fabulous new author!

Guaranteed to brighten your day is SHARING SUNRISE by Judy Gill, LOVESWEPT #485. This utterly delightful story features a heroine who's determined to settle down with the only man she has ever wanted . . . except the dashing, virile object of her affection doesn't believe her love has staying power. Marian Crane can't deny that as a youth she was filled with wanderlust, but Rolph McKenzie must realize that now she's ready to commit herself for keeps. This handsome hunk is wary, but he gives her a job as his assistant at the marina—and soon discovers the delicious thrill of her womanly charms. Dare he believe that her eyes glitter not with excitement over faraway places but with promise of forever? You'll relish this delectable treat from Judy Gill.

And be sure to look for our FANFARE novels next month—three thrilling historicals with vastly different settings and times. Ask your bookseller for A LASTING FIRE by the bestselling author of THE MORGAN WOMEN, Beverly Byrne, IN THE SHADOW OF THE MOUNTAIN by the beloved Rosanne Bittner, and THE BONNIE BLUE by LOVESWEPT's own Joan Elliott Pickart.

Happy reading!

With every good wish,

Carolyn Nichols

Carolyn Nichols
Publisher, FANFARE and LOVESWEPT

60 Minutes to a Better, More Beautiful You!

Now it's easier than ever to awaken your sensuality, stay slim forever—even make yourself irresistible. With Bantam's bestselling subliminal audio tapes, you're only 60 minutes away from a better, more beautiful you!

___ 45004-2	**Slim Forever**	....	$8.95
___ 45035-2	**Stop Smoking Forever**	....	$8.95
___ 45022-0	**Positively Change Your Life**	...	$8.95
___ 45041-7	**Stress Free Forever**	....	$8.95
___ 45106-5	**Get a Good Night's Sleep**	....	$7.95
___ 45094-8	**Improve Your Concentration**	.	$7.95
___ 45172-3	**Develop A Perfect Memory**	.....	$8.95

NEW!

Handsome Book Covers Specially Designed To Fit Loveswept Books

Our new French Calf Vinyl book covers come in a set of three great colors—royal blue, scarlet red and kachina green.

Each 7" × 9½" book cover has two deep vertical pockets, a handy sewn-in bookmark, and is soil and scratch resistant.

To order your set, use the form below.